EYES ON THE GOAL

EYES
ON THE
GOAL

JOHN COY

FEIWEL AND FRIENDS
NEW YORK

A FEIWEL AND FRIENDS BOOK
An Imprint of Macmillan

Coy, John,
Eyes on the goal / John Coy. — 1st ed.
p. cm.
Summary: Middle-schooler Jackson's baseball skills are not of much help
when he and his friends go to soccer camp, and while there he learns that his
mother's boyfriend has invited them to move into his house, and friend
Gig's father is deployed to Afghanistan.
ISBN: 978-0-312-37330-6
[1. Soccer—Fiction.   2. Camps—Fiction.   3. Ability—Fiction.
4. Friendship—Fiction.   5. Soldiers—Fiction.   6. Family life—Fiction.]
I. Title.
PZ7.C839455Eye 2010
[Fic]—dc22
2009045387

Book design by Tim Hall

Feiwel and Friends logo designed by Filomena Tuosto

First Edition: 2010

10 9 8 7 6 5 4 3 2 1

www.feiwelandfriends.com

For Alastair

CHAPTER 1

I pump the pedals of my bike as I race to Gig's house. The breeze cools my face, and the sun's still high in the sky. Summer rocks. No school. No getting up early. And days that feel like they'll last forever.

I lift my hands from the handlebars and sit up straight. Freedom. That's what August is. No boring homework. No teachers and parents watching every move. Freedom to do what we want on a Friday night.

At Gig's house, I lean my bike against the basketball hoop and climb the cement steps. The chimes of the doorbell echo in the house. Footsteps approach and the door opens.

"Hi, Jackson," Gig's sister, Sydney, answers. "Come on in."

"Hey, Syd." She's wearing short shorts and a white tank top that shows off her tan. Her brown hair is held back in a thin headband. She looks more like a beach girl than the tough second baseman I played with on the Panthers last spring.

"How are you doing?" she asks.

"Umm, fine."

She looks at me like I'll say more. I've known her six years now—as long as I've known Gig—but lately I get tongue-tied around her. Part of it is that she's really smart. Part of it is that she's Gig's sister. But the main reason is that I'm not very good at talking to girls.

"When you and Gig are at soccer camp," she says, "my mom and I are going to have fun."

I stick my hands in the pockets of my cargo shorts and stand there like a dork. I don't know what to say so I just kind of nod.

"Gig's in his room," Sydney says. "Probably killing something in some video game."

"Okay." I don't know why talking to girls has gotten harder. When I was younger I used to be able to do it fine.

Gig's got a new sign on his door:

STOP! KEEP OUT!
THIS MEANS YOU!
ABSOLUTELY NO TRESPASSING!
YOU'VE BEEN WARNED! YES, THIS MEANS YOU!

It means Sydney, not me, so I knock.

"Die, zombie scum," Gig shouts over the noise of massive explosions.

"It's me, Jackson."

"Open the door, then."

Gig's sitting shirtless with his hair sticking out in different directions, blasting zombies left and right.

"What are you playing?"

"Extreme Zombie Invasion." Gig's eyes are locked on the screen. "I'm going to finally get to the Supreme Commander level."

I brush off boxers, two towels, and a bunch of video game cases and sit in the chair. My room's a mess, but it's nothing compared to this. Clothes, shoes, and empty Doritos bags cover the floor.

"Have you started packing yet?" I don't see a bag.

"What for?"

"Soccer camp."

"I'm not going." Gig stays focused on the screen.

"What? You promised Diego, Isaac, and me that you'd go. Remember our deal with Diego to do this so he'll play football with us? You can't break it."

"That was before my dad left for National Guard training." Gig wipes out three more zombies. "When Dad left, he said I was the man of the house now."

Gig's fingers fly at the controls. Like blasting zombies in a video game keeps his mom and Sydney safe.

"Gig, you have to come. We're signed up to room together. I don't want some loser roomie."

"Maybe they'll let you have a single."

"I don't want a single." He can be so stupid sometimes. "I'm not crazy about soccer, either, but we all agreed we'd go to camp."

"It's not about soccer." Gig looks over at me. "I can't go."

Dun, dun da dunn. "Sorry, loser, you failed." A zombie screeches. "Try again."

"Stop messing me up," Gig shouts. "I was almost there."

"Let's go to Isaac's. He and Diego said to come over."

"No way," Gig says. "I'm staying here until I beat this dumb game."

"Well, I'm not." I get up and kick his baseball glove out

of the way. "You promised you'd go to camp. We all did. You can't back out now."

Gig doesn't even look up.

Diego and Isaac are kicking a soccer ball in the backyard of Isaac's house. Sweat glistens on Isaac's dark skin and Diego's got a new buzz cut.

"Hey, what took you so long?" Isaac boots the ball to me and it skims across the thick grass.

"I was at Gig's." I kick it to Diego.

"Ready for camp?" Diego passes the ball back to me. He's big and strong, but he moves smoothly.

"Almost." I slide the ball back and forth between my feet.

"We're going to have a blast." Isaac wipes his face with his Lakers T-shirt. "There's a girl's camp at the same time."

I tap a pass to him. "Sweet."

"We'll meet a bunch of new girls." Isaac tries a pass, but the ball hits a tree. "Maybe we'll even get you a girlfriend."

I track down the ball. Yeah, right. I'm having trouble even *talking* to girls. "We've got a problem."

"What?" Isaac and Diego say together.

"Gig's not coming." I pass to Diego, who traps it.

"Why not?" he asks. "He promised."

"He has to come," Isaac says.

"I know, but he says since his dad's gone, he has to stay home."

"Did his dad really say that?" Diego drills me a pass.

I dribble the ball around the birdbath. "He said Gig's the man of the house."

"Gig's the man?" Isaac laughs. "That's one house I'm staying out of."

"He promised," Diego repeats.

"Let's take some shots." Isaac steals the ball from me and faces the side of the garage. "Who's goalie?"

"I am." Diego grabs two lawn chairs and sets them on each side. "Give me your best shot."

I push Isaac off the ball and kick a low shot that Diego swats away.

"Is that all you've got?" he taunts. "My grandma shoots harder than that."

"Those chairs are too close." I pull one out a couple of feet.

"They're fine where they are." Diego pulls it back.

Isaac lines up and sizzles a shot wide that smacks off the garage.

I rebound the miss and rush toward Diego. I fake a shot

and he leans left. I turn and blast the ball just inside the chair. "He shoots! He scores!" I raise my arms above my head. "GOOOOOAL!"

Even without Gig, I'm excited about soccer camp.

Chapter 2

Saturday morning, I sit up front with Mom as we drive to the farmer's market with Quinn, my six-year-old brother.

"I've got a lot to get today," she says. "You boys have to help carry the bags."

"We'll need doughnuts first," I say.

"Doughnuts, doughnuts," Quinn echoes from the back.

"Okay, you can each get a doughnut." Mom stops at a light and checks her face in the mirror. She puckers her lips and dabs at a spot of lipstick. "I'm making a special dinner tomorrow night for Ted's birthday. Heather and Haley will come, too. I want everything to be perfect."

I check the street for a parking spot. That's the best reason yet to go to soccer camp. I won't have to be here for Mom's boyfriend's birthday and pretend to be nice to his girls.

"There's one." I point to a silver pickup pulling out.

Mom backs in smoothly. She opens her door and takes a deep breath. "I can already smell flowers."

I step onto the sidewalk. All I smell is exhaust from the old truck.

Ahead of us, two dogs, one big and one small, sniff around each other.

"A wiener dog." Quinn points. "Can I pet him?"

"Ask the owner first," Mom says.

Quinn runs up to a short bald man who seems pleased Quinn chose his dog over the German shepherd.

"Are you excited about soccer camp?" Mom presses the remote to lock the doors.

"Yeah, kind of. But Gig's not coming." I kick a stone on the sidewalk.

"Why not?"

"I don't know. He's acting weird."

"Well, that's too bad, but I'm sure you'll have a good time anyway. Saint Boniface is supposed to be a beautiful campus."

I kick the stone again and it skids along the concrete and narrowly misses the wiener dog.

"That's enough, Jackson," Mom warns.

"You like dogs, don't you?" the bald guy says to Quinn.

"I love dogs!" Quinn rubs the wiener dog behind the ears. "But my mommy's allergic."

"That's too bad," the man says, as he looks at Mom and me and then back to Quinn like that's the saddest thing in the history of the world.

"We've got to get going," Mom says. Across the street, tables of the farmer's market are piled high with fruits, vegetables, and flowers. "Look at all those colors," Mom says. "It looks like a painting."

"Look at all those doughnuts." I point to the stand. "I'm in heaven."

"Let's go there first." Quinn looks up at me.

When the lights turn, we hurry past eggplants, peppers, and zucchini to the table filled with doughnuts: glazed, sprinkled, chocolate, jelly-filled—every doughnut you can think of. Behind them, wearing a long apron, a baker's hat, and her long hair in braids is the Doughnut Lady.

"One glazed, one chocolate with sprinkles," I order.

"That's for you and Quinn, right?" Mom asks.

I shake my head. "No, just for me. I've got to stock up. They might not have doughnuts at camp."

Quinn copies me and orders the same, and we munch away as we trail behind Mom, who picks out one vegetable after another. "Isn't that your teacher, Mrs. Spanier?" Mom looks down the long row of tables.

At the end, Mrs. Spanier, who Gig and I call Snuffy, examines a cantaloupe and sets it back. "Yeah, let's go the other way."

"Absolutely not, Jackson," Mom says firmly. "It won't kill you to go down and say hello to your teacher."

"She's not my teacher anymore." I lick chocolate off my finger. "She's my ex-teacher."

Mom gives me a poke in the back and I march forward.

"Hello, Mrs. Spanier," Mom calls out cheerfully.

"Why, hello, Mrs. Kennedy." Snuffy smiles. "How nice to see you. Jackson, are you enjoying your summer?"

"Yeah." I wipe my hands on my cargo shorts and look down. Snuffy always makes me feel like I've done something wrong.

"And is this your little brother?" She bends down to Quinn's eye level. "What's your name?"

"Quinn," he says louder than necessary.

"What a lovely name. What grade are you in?"

"I'm going to be in first." He holds up one finger.

"Good for you. I hope I'm lucky enough to have you in fifth grade in a few years."

"Jackson." She stands up. "I was watching the ball game last night and thought about that story you wrote last spring about the baseball superhero. What was his name? Homerun Hero?"

"Homerunzilla."

"That was a great story. With ideas like that, you'll do fine in middle school."

"Uh, thanks." I'm shocked. Snuffy doesn't give many compliments. Not to me anyway. While she and Mom share secrets for super-moist zucchini bread, I watch her. She's got her regular pointed glasses, but her face looks more relaxed. She's even smiling like a regular person. Maybe she likes summer better than school, too. Maybe she's more like me than I ever imagined.

Saturday afternoon, I meet Dad at the park for some soccer practice before camp. I sit on the bleachers tying the laces of my new cleats. Dad sits next to me stretching out his long legs. He's got brown hair and green eyes like me, but his ears don't stick out like mine. Maybe they won't look so big when I'm older.

"I picked up something for you." Dad hands me a bag from Fat Tony's Sport Mart.

"What is it?" I open the bag and pull out two Under Armour shirts, a blue one and a gray one.

"They're those wick-away shirts that move sweat away from the body. You might have some hot days up there."

"Thanks." I rub the fabric between my fingers. "I like them."

"Good," Dad says. "Let's get started. An important part of soccer is stretching." He raises his arms above his head. "It keeps you flexible and helps prevent injuries."

He sounds like Coach Wilkins from baseball, who always had us stretch.

"Let's do a few together." Dad and I walk to the outfield grass. He sits down and stretches one leg in front of him and bends the other one back. He rubs his eyes. He looks tired from working late last night at his job as a chef. "Put your hands beside your leg and slowly bend down."

I place my hands beside my knee and lean forward.

"Use your breathing," Dad says. "When you exhale, relax deeper into the stretch."

He says stuff like this ever since he started taking yoga at the Y. I don't really understand what he means, but I try to lean farther forward.

"Relax," Dad says. "Let gravity do some of the work of pulling you down."

Yeah, right. I bend my head and examine blades of grass. After we've finished stretching, we kick the ball around in the outfield.

"Drive the ball with the instep of your foot." Dad demonstrates a strong kick.

"Did you play varsity soccer in high school?" I chase the ball down.

"For a year," Dad says. "Then I got a coach who was so intense that he took the fun out of it, so I quit."

"What did your dad say?"

"He didn't like it." Dad dribbles the ball. "But I wasn't going to do something I didn't want to. I just played for fun after that." He boots a high bouncer and I stick my hand out to stop it.

"No hands," Dad calls.

"I know. I know." In all the games I love—baseball, football, basketball—you use your hands. Why would somebody invent a game where you can't use your hands?

Dad shows me how to use my foot to trap a bouncing ball. He shows me how to fake going one way and then go the other. He teaches me to do toe taps and circle toe taps so that I touch the ball with the tip of one foot and then the other in a hoppity dance. "You're a good athlete," he says. "You'll do fine."

"But some of the kids at camp will have been playing soccer since they could stand up. I'll be way behind."

"Don't worry," Dad says. "You're there to have fun. It's not a competition."

That's where he's wrong. Once we get to camp, I'm sure it will be a competition.

CHAPTER 3

I bike down the long driveway at Mom's house—really Liz and Jeff's house, Mom's friends who are in Italy. We're house-sitting for them, which is like babysitting their house, while they're gone. I park my bike in the garage, and Mom opens the door and comes down the steps.

"Good news. Ted got last-minute tickets to an outdoor orchestra concert tonight." She smiles. "We can have a picnic and listen to music."

"Mom, I can't go. I've got to pack for camp."

"That won't take long." She bends down and picks a couple of leaves out of her pot of petunias. "You can pack and clean up now. You'll have time before Ted and the girls come to pick us up at six."

"I don't *want* to go." I wipe the sleeve of my T-shirt across my forehead.

"This is a special opportunity to see the orchestra. Besides, it's our last chance to all be together before you go to camp. And you can wish Ted an early happy birthday."

"But I need to get ready for camp."

"Jackson, Ted made a special trip down to the box office and stood in line to get tickets. I don't want you to disappoint him by not showing up after he's gone to all that trouble."

"FINE!" I stomp up the steps like a sumo wrestler.

*I*n my room, I find my checklist of items to pack for St. Boniface Soccer Camp. I pull my duffel bag out of the closet and throw in shorts, shirts, a swimsuit, and a towel.

"What are you doing?" Quinn scampers in the open door and follows me around. Sometimes he even acts like a puppy.

"Packing for camp." I grab my cell phone from my dresser.

Quinn turns to leave. He's wearing black pants, a button-down purple shirt, and his hair is neatly gelled.

"Wait, Quinn." I wave him back. "I thought I had more time, but now I've got to hurry up because of this stupid concert." I grab socks, underwear, and a sweatshirt.

"What about this?" Quinn picks up my baseball hat from the floor.

"Oh, yeah." I throw it in the bag.

I check my list again and grab my toothbrush, toothpaste, deodorant, and shampoo from the bathroom. I pull my phone charger from the outlet and pack it.

"How long will you be gone?" Quinn sticks to me like a shadow.

"Just a week. I'll be back Friday afternoon."

Quinn sticks out his bottom lip.

"It'll go fast." I jam the stuff down in my bag. "We can get ice cream at Sunny's when I get back."

Mom walks into the room. "How's your packing coming?"

"I need sunscreen and bug spray."

"There should be some of both in the bathroom cupboard. Did you pack deodorant?"

"Yes, Mom."

"Enough clean underwear?"

"No, Mom. I decided to bring dirty."

Quinn bursts out laughing and snorts like a pig. Mom shakes her head. "Remember to call me from camp."

"Okay."

"Look at this beautiful postcard of Sicily from Liz and Jeff." She holds up a picture of a temple with columns. "Greek ruins of Agrigento," she reads from the back. "I'd love to go to Italy someday." She reads the rest of the card. "Liz and Jeff are traveling for a month and they'll return here in September."

"To this house?" Quinn asks.

"Of course," Mom says. "This is their house."

"Will we stay here, too?" Quinn looks confused.

"No." Mom shakes her head. "We'll get our own place."

"But this house is really big." Quinn spreads out his arms as wide as he can.

"Jeff works at home." Mom bends down and gives Quinn a hug. "He's a composer and he needs quiet. Besides, it will be great to have our own place."

"Where?" I look over at her and she gives me a weak smile.

"I don't know yet," she says, "but don't worry. I'll take care of it."

I go into the bathroom and search the shelves for sunscreen and bug spray. Of course I want to know where I'm going to be living half the time next month.

"Put on some nice clothes after you shower, Jackson," Mom says. "No shorts. No jeans."

"Mom, it's a picnic."

"A picnic with the orchestra, a cultural opportunity. I'm

sure Heather and Haley will be dressed nicely." She puts her hand on Quinn's shoulder as they leave the room.

I check the list again. I've got everything except the cleats and shin guards, which are at Dad's house.

Still, it feels like something is missing. Gig. I wish I could stuff him in my bag and bring him to camp.

When Ted picks us up, we crowd into his Chrysler.

"Jackson, you sit up front." Mom loads the picnic basket and blankets into the trunk. "Quinn, you get in back."

"I guess I need to get a bigger car." Ted flashes his shiny grin.

Haley, who's six, is whispering to Heather about not wanting the middle. I get in the front seat next to Mom and roll down the window.

"No need, Jackson," Ted calls. "I've got the AC on."

I roll the window back up. It's really nice out. I'd rather have fresh air.

Heather, who's a little older than me, has her long legs scrunched up in the middle. She's wearing a dress and I smell her flowery perfume. Every time I see her, she's all dressed up. Does she ever wear normal clothes?

"Tonight the orchestra will perform Ravel's *Boléro*," Mom

says. "The rhythm gets faster and faster until it is so fast you can't believe it can go any faster."

"And then it does," Heather says.

"And then they'll play the *1812 Overture*," Ted says. "With a real cannon blast."

Big deal. I stare out the window as we pass kids carrying baseball gloves and a bat. That's what I'd rather be doing instead of being trapped in here.

At the park, Mom finds a space on the hill and spreads out the plaid blankets on the grass. The park is already packed with people.

Mom unloads items from the basket and hands me a stack of napkins. "Jackson, pass one of these to everyone. Quinn, you pass out the plates."

"Okay, Mom." Quinn hands each person a yellow plastic plate.

I follow, handing out matching napkins with sunflowers on them.

Heather sets a paper cup at each place and Haley lays out plastic forks and knives.

Mom and Ted work together, pulling food from the basket: roasted chicken, potato salad, coleslaw, carrots, spinach dip, chips, guacamole, string cheese, and double chocolate chip cookies.

"What a feast." Ted helps Haley pull off the top of the dip.

"Such a beautiful evening for a concert," Mom says.

Suddenly I'm starving. I take a bite of a drumstick.

Heather looks over at me. "I hear you're going to camp tomorrow."

"Yeah." I wipe my mouth with my napkin.

"I go to camp in a week," she says.

"What kind of camp?" I take a drink of lemonade. I can't imagine her at any camp other than dress-up camp.

"Canoe camp. We plan a two-week trip into the wilderness with our counselors." She sets some carrots on her plate. "Where are you going?"

"Soccer camp at Saint Boniface."

"Just boys?" She tucks her hair back.

"No, boys and girls. We're on separate teams, stay in separate dorms, but we're at camp at the same time."

"That's like ours. Girls and boys go on separate trips, but we're in camp together at the beginning and end."

"Where do you sleep?"

"Cabins in camp and sleeping bags in tents on the trail."

I look over at her long, skinny arms. She doesn't look

strong enough to paddle a canoe or carry a pack. "What do you eat on the trip?"

"We pack in our food and take turns cooking. Lots of spaghetti, polenta, and rice," she says. "Sometimes we catch fish and fry them up. It depends if any of the girls are vegetarian. Where do you eat?"

"In the Dining Center. All we do is show up and eat. Kind of like this." I reach for a chip, dip it in guacamole, and pop it in my mouth.

Heather leans back and her hoop earrings sparkle as she turns her head. It's hard to believe that in a week she'll be paddling a canoe through the wilderness.

"What do you do for showers?"

"We jump in the lake." She passes me the string cheese.

"What about, you know . . ."

"What?" The corners of her mouth turn up.

"The bathroom."

She laughs. "Haven't you ever been in the woods? We go just like the other animals. Only we cover ours up."

She peels thin strings off her cheese and puts them in her mouth. Girls sure surprise you sometimes.

CHAPTER 4

At Dad's house on Sunday morning, Quinn and I help in the kitchen while G-Man, my grandpa who doesn't like to be called Grandpa, sets the table. I rub a chunk of cheddar over the cheese grater and sample a piece that's fallen on the cutting board.

"I ran into Nick Sportelli, Sam's dad, at Kwik Trip yesterday." G-Man picks out the silverware. "He said the baseball traveling team struggled this year."

I lift off the grater to see how high the pile of cheese is and take another sample. G-Man wanted me to go out for the traveling team this spring, but I didn't. I wish he would quit bringing it up.

"Sam was a backup infielder and didn't get to play much." G-Man folds a napkin in a triangle and sets the fork on top.

If Sam didn't play much, I sure wouldn't have, either.

"Nick says Sam hated riding the bench." G-Man shifts a plate so all four line up.

"I would, too." I brush the last bits of cheese from the grater. I'm glad I played with my friends on the Panthers. After a rough start, we finished second in the league. And I had fun playing with Isaac, Diego, Gig, and even Gig's sister, Sydney, who joined us and turned out to be pretty good.

"Looks like you made a good call on that." G-Man takes the glasses out of the cupboard.

Dad looks up from slicing mushrooms and nods at me.

"Thanks, G-Man." I hand Dad the plate of cheese. G-Man doesn't admit he's wrong very often.

After our breakfast of omelets, toast, and strawberries, I double-check my list and add the shin guards and cleats to my bag. I go through my shirts and pick out three of my favorites: the two new Under Armours from Dad, and the black one with the basketball on it that reads GO STRONG.

"Ten minutes until we go get Isaac," Dad calls.

"We'll leave when you do." I hear G-Man. "Quinn and I are going to the pool."

"Then for ice cream," Quinn says, jumping up and down.

As I'm zipping up my bag, my phone rings. Must be Mom with one last reminder. I pull the phone out of my pocket and check the screen. It's not Mom. It's Gig.

"Yeah?"

"Hey." His voice is quieter.

"What's up?"

"I'm . . . I'm coming to camp."

"You are?" I lift my bag off my bed.

"Can you pick me up?"

"Awesome. What happened?"

"My mom and dad double-teamed me. Mom said she and Sydney could manage without me for a week. Dad called this morning and said I should go. Besides, they've already paid for camp and don't want the money wasted."

"Do you have cleats and everything you need for camp?"

"Everything except shin guards."

"Maybe they'll have some at camp. We'll pick you up in fifteen minutes."

I shut the phone and then have an idea. I dial Diego's number.

"Hello."

"Hey, Diego. Are you still at home?"

"Yeah. What's up?"

"Great news. I talked to Gig. He's coming to camp. We'll all meet you up there."

"Like we promised. We'll all be together."

"Hey, do you have an extra pair of shin guards?" I carry my bag into the living room.

"My brother might. Why?"

"Gig needs them."

"I'll check," Diego says. "My uncle and cousins just got here. Gotta go. See you at camp."

On the drive up, I sit in front with Dad, while Isaac and Gig are in back.

"Do you think Diego is better at soccer than he is at baseball?" Isaac asks.

"No way," Gig says. "He was an all-star in baseball."

I turn around to talk with them. "Yeah, but he's great in soccer, too." Gig's wearing his favorite T-shirt, the one with an arrow, which says I'M WITH STUPID. The arrow points straight to Isaac.

"He's good at everything," Isaac says. "I'm glad he's playing football with us next month when we start middle school."

Gig covers his ears. "Don't even talk about school. I don't want to think about it."

"Diego told me his cousin is better at soccer than he is," Isaac says.

"What's his cousin's name?" I ask.

"Don't know." Isaac shakes his head. "He never said."

I stare out the window at a collapsing barn. Nobody has used that in a really long time.

"How's your dad doing, Gig?" Dad looks up in the rearview mirror.

"Okay," Gig says quickly. "He says training in August in Mississippi is like living inside a furnace. He misses summer here."

"I bet," Dad says. "How much longer is he there?"

"Ten days," Gig says.

"Then to Afghanistan?" Dad asks.

"Yeah." Gig looks out the window.

Dad adjusts the AC vent. "Let us know if we can help out. Call anytime for a ride or anything else."

We drive past a lake where algae have taken over. Green goo covers the surface. After all this sitting, I'm ready for camp. I need to run around.

We pull off the highway and follow the brown arrow to the left that reads ST. BONIFACE COLLEGE. The road dips down between curtains of pine trees on either side. Dad rolls down the window and the scent of the woods fills the car.

"I'm starving," Gig announces.

I look over at the clock. "We don't eat for a couple hours."

We drive past a lake where boys are fishing from the shore. The water looks cool and clean.

"I feel like jumping in right now," Isaac says.

"Me, too."

"Not me." Gig makes a face. "Fish poop in that lake."

Isaac and I laugh and so does Dad.

The road curves up to a four-way stop where a big sign announces:

WELCOME TO ST. BONIFACE COLLEGE AND ABBEY

"What's an abbey?" Gig asks.

"A place where monks live," Dad says.

"What are monks?" Gig says. "Some kind of baby monkey?"

Dad turns around to look at him like he can't believe he's serious. "Monks are members of a religious order who live together. Some of the monks teach at the college. Others have different jobs."

A white-haired man waves as he steps cautiously into the crosswalk. He's wearing a tan short-sleeved shirt and black pants pulled up way too high.

"That man's probably a monk." Dad waits patiently for him to cross.

"But he's not wearing robes," Isaac says.

"They don't wear robes all the time," Dad says. "They're free to wear what they want."

"Like high-water pants," Gig says, and we all crack up.

As we drive onto campus, six boys are standing in a circle in the shade of a tree. They're keeping a soccer ball in the air with their knees, feet, and heads. They goof around and make it look so easy. I couldn't do that in a million years.

Beside them, a boy in a tie-dyed T-shirt lifts his leg and balances the ball on his foot. I didn't even know that was possible.

There's no way I can play with these guys. What's Diego gotten us into?

CHAPTER 5

Boys and girls crowd around the registration table in the Student Commons to get their room assignments and key cards. Isaac and I follow Gig, who goes around to the side while Dad stands in back. We get stuck behind a bunch of girls in matching orange soccer jerseys. I knew there would be girls here, but I didn't realize there would be this many.

"Excuse me." Gig raises his hand and uses his polite voice.

A woman with short blond hair, who's wearing a St. Bonnie's shirt, looks up. She must be a college student here.

"Last name is Milroy," Gig says.

The woman scans her sheet. "Spencer Milroy." She checks off his name.

"Not Spencer. Gig Milroy," he says. "Cross out the Spencer. G. I. G."

The woman marks her paper. "Room 345, Benedict Hall,

Gig." She smiles and hands him a key card. "Is your room-mate here?"

"Yep." I step forward. "Jackson Kennedy."

"Welcome to soccer camp, Jackson." She hands me my key card. "Hang on to these. There's a charge if you lose them."

I put the card in my pocket.

"Here's your packet." She hands Gig and me green folders that have St. Boniface printed on them in old-fashioned letters. "This contains the schedule and everything else you'll need to know. Dinner is at six in the Dining Center. Let me know if you have any questions."

"Just one," says Gig.

"Yes?"

"What's your name?"

"Lauren." She laughs.

"Thanks, Lauren." Gig shakes her hand. "I'm Gig. Pleased to meet you."

"Gig. Got it," Lauren says.

Isaac rolls his eyes at me and steps forward. "Isaac Wilkins," he says.

Gig leans over to me and whispers, "She's into me."

"Who?"

"Lauren, you dummy."

"Gig, she's a college student."

"I know," he says. "I can't help it if older girls dig me."

"Yeah, it must be your maturity."

When Isaac has his key, I move forward. "Has Diego Jimenez checked in yet?"

She runs her finger down the list. "No, not yet. We're still waiting for a number of campers."

"See you around, Lauren." Gig waves.

Dad helps us locate Benedict Hall on our map. "That's close enough to walk," he says.

We all get our duffel bags out of the back.

"Nice campus," Dad says.

Old brick buildings are covered with vines, and purple and gold flowers bloom in beds along the sidewalk.

Gig shifts his bag and a pair of red-white-and-blue boxer shorts falls out. Dad bends down and hands them to him. "Very patriotic."

"Thanks, Mr. K." Gig sets them on his head.

I turn to Isaac. "What room do you and Diego have?"

"Room 352 Benedict Hall," he says. "We must be close to you."

"It's beautiful up here," Dad says. "I think you'll have a great time."

"I hope the soccer isn't too intense," I say. "Other than Diego, none of us have played much."

"I'm sure they'll have players of all abilities," Dad says. "You'll do fine."

The six guys who were kicking the ball under the tree cross in front of us. They look even bigger close up. I hope I don't have to go up against any of them. I hope they're not in my group.

"Nice hat," the biggest guy says to Gig.

"Thanks." He waves.

We open a heavy door and climb the stairs to the third floor. We open another door and walk down a long, dark-tiled hall. At the end, we turn left and follow the numbers to Room 345.

Our room has two beds, two desks, two towels, two washcloths—two of everything. It reminds me of Noah's ark.

"I call this side." Gig plops down on the bed next to the window.

"You've got a nice view." Dad looks out the window at big maple trees and rolling hills.

I set my bag on the other bed and look around. The white

walls are completely bare. It's not what I expected of a college dorm. I imagined posters, pictures, and lots of color, but there's nothing. Of course it's the summer and the students aren't here, but the room feels more like a prison cell.

I slide open the closet door and set my T-shirts on the shelf. Dad keeps looking out the window like he's not sure what to do next.

"Well, you two look all set," he says. "I should be getting back."

I throw my underwear in a drawer. I wish Dad wouldn't leave right away. Gig's lying on his bed staring up at the ceiling. I bet he's thinking about his dad.

"Have a good week." Dad walks to the door. "Mr. Wilkins will pick you up on Friday."

"Okay." I take a step back. I hope Dad gets the hint that I don't want any hugging stuff in front of Gig.

"Yeah, thanks, Mr. K." Gig sits up. "We're going to rule this place."

Dad waves as he walks out the door. "Have fun." I listen to his footsteps echo down the hall.

After we've unpacked, Isaac, Gig, and I head outside.

"Look at all these hot girls," Gig says.

"I'm looking." Isaac eyes the group of four walking toward us.

The girls, who are wearing shorts and tight T-shirts, come closer. They're talking excitedly and one with long blond hair walks in front of Isaac and smiles. "Hi."

"Hey," he says, and keeps walking.

"Ladies." Gig lifts his hand as they pass.

I glance back at them giggling and whispering.

"They're into us," Gig says.

"One for each of us," Isaac adds.

"I can take two," Gig says.

"I was counting Diego, you dope." Isaac pushes Gig into a flower bed.

"What he doesn't know won't hurt him." Gig hops among the gold flowers.

The church bells clang five times.

"How come Diego isn't here yet?"

"You've got a cell phone," Gig says. "Call him."

I pull my phone out of my pocket. "I don't know if I'll get a signal up here."

"It's a college," Isaac says, "not the moon."

I press Diego's number and the call goes through.

"Yeah?"

"Diego, where are you?"

"We're at the sign-up desk." I hear his family talking in the background and give Isaac and Gig a thumbs-up.

"We're on our way." I snap the phone shut and we race each other to the door of the Student Commons. Gig gets there first, but Isaac puts his hand on the door so it can't open. Gig pulls and pulls, and then Isaac lets go. Gig falls backward on his butt, and Isaac and I jump down the stairs.

"Diego!" I holler as we rush through the crowd like we haven't seen him in years.

"This is my family," he says. "My dad, my mom, my uncle, my aunt, my cousins." He points to two boys and a girl.

I lift my hand in a wave and the adults smile.

"These are my friends Isaac and Jackson," Diego says. "And Gig." Gig gives Isaac a push and stands next to me.

Diego's aunt asks his mom something in Spanish and we stand around awkwardly.

"You're in Room 352 with me," Isaac says.

"I know." Diego holds up his key card.

"Which one of your cousins is the big soccer player?" Gig asks.

The two boys stand close to their mom. Neither one of them looks big enough to be here at camp.

"I am." The girl steps forward.

I stare at her. She has long black hair and brown eyes with dark lashes.

"I'm Angela," she says as our eyes meet.

Gig moves closer. "I'm Gig."

"She already knows who we are," Isaac says. "Diego just introduced us."

Gig whacks his forehead like he's got memory problems.

Angela's beautiful. She's the soccer star we've been hearing about? Why didn't Diego tell us about her?

CHAPTER 6

"**Y**ou can go back as much as you want." Gig digs into his mashed potatoes at dinner. "Seconds, thirds, whatever."

"We get the idea." Isaac cuts his turkey. He's sitting between Gig and me, while Angela and Diego sit across from us. The Dining Center is big, with brick walls dividing it up into smaller sections. Large windows open onto a garden in the interior courtyard.

I glance up at Angela. She's got high cheekbones and smooth skin. I try to think up something cool to say but come up empty.

"And you can have as much to drink as you want." Gig finishes off his Mountain Dew and slams it on his tray. "Dessert, too. All you can eat."

"You sound like you're at food camp," Isaac says.

"I am." Gig grins. "I told you I wasn't into soccer."

"You don't like soccer?" Angela looks up with her big brown eyes.

"Nah." Gig slices up his turkey "It's kind of boring."

"He's just kidding." Diego turns to Angela.

"No, I'm not," Gig says. "Compared to other sports, soccer *is* boring."

"Are you crazy?" Angela stares across the table at him. "Soccer is the best game in the world—all the players working together to guard their goal and passing the ball to score. There's absolutely nothing better."

She waves her hands as she talks. I hope they keep arguing so I can continue watching her.

"There's nothing sweeter than a well-played goal," she says.

"Whatever." Gig picks up his plate. "I need more meat. Anybody else going for seconds?"

"No, I'm good." I wave him off.

"I want to check out the dessert bar." Isaac turns toward the glass cases where plates of cakes and pies are lined up.

I lean forward toward Angela. "Umm, what grade are you going to be in?"

"Sixth." She finishes her cranberry juice. "How about you?"

"Same. Middle school. With Diego." I try to think of something else to talk about. "How long have you been playing soccer?"

"Since I could walk." She smiles. "My dad loves soccer and Diego's dad loves baseball. Even though they're brothers, they're very different."

Diego nods. "That's true."

"How long have you played soccer?" Angela asks.

"Not as long as you have. Baseball was my first sport. I played a lot with my grandpa. And then I played football and basketball. But my dad's favorite sport is soccer. I like it, too."

"But your dad didn't teach you soccer first?"

"No, he's not like that. He let me choose."

"My dad's not that way." Angela shakes her head.

"Definitely not," Diego says.

"My dad's coached me in soccer since I was little. He always pushes me to be the best because he wants me to earn a college soccer scholarship." She stands up and picks up her glass. "I need more juice. Do you want anything?"

"No, I'm good." As she walks away, I realize I should have thought of something to ask her to bring me. Better yet, I should have gone with her. I always think of these things too late.

41

"Gig's wrong about soccer." Diego scoops up his last bite of potatoes. "We're going to have fun at camp."

"Yeah," I say. "How come you never told us your cousin was a girl?"

Diego looks up and smiles. "You never asked."

After dinner, we have half an hour before the first scheduled activity, so we check out the campus. A cobblestone path winds under an archway and we follow the uneven stones. On the right is a fountain surrounded by flowers and a sign that reads:

MONASTIC GARDENS: DO NOT ENTER

Ahead of us is a huge church with two towers.

"Let's see if it's open." Diego climbs the steps and opens the door.

We all file in and Diego and Angela dip their hands in holy water and make the sign of the cross. The evening light streams through the blue-and-gold stained-glass windows.

Diego whispers something to Angela and they go to a side chapel. Diego digs some change out of his pocket and the coins clang into a metal box. Angela flicks a match and lights a candle.

I turn to Gig. "What are they doing?"

"Beats me," he says. "I don't know anything about this stuff."

"I think it's a prayer for someone who's sick or someone who's died," Isaac says.

"What good is praying for someone who's already dead?" Gig asks.

"I don't know," Isaac says. "Ask Diego."

I sit down in one of the black wooden pews and look at the painted figures of Jesus, Mary, and Joseph behind the altar. Neither Mom nor Dad goes to church regularly, but I like sitting here. I feel a little quieter and a little calmer.

Camp is going to be fine.

All the campers are gathered in the gym for the welcome and introduction. On the bleachers, Angela sits between Diego and me as we wait for the first speaker.

"Let's get this show on the road," Gig says. "Check it out. There's Lauren."

Lauren goes up to the microphone and taps on it a couple of times. "Testing. Testing. One, two, three."

"You pass," Gig yells out.

She sees him and waves. A short guy with a shaved head and whistle around his neck walks up and takes the microphone from Lauren. He puts one hand out and waits for everybody to be quiet.

"Welcome, soccer campers, to Saint Boniface," he says in a deep voice. "I'm Coach Derek, your camp director."

I look down at Angela's feet, which are crossed at the ankles. She's wearing brown flip-flops, a white ankle bracelet, and pink polish on her toenails.

"We don't have many rules here at camp," Coach says. "But the ones we do have, we expect you to follow."

I wonder if Angela polished her toenails for camp.

"The most important rule is to be on time," Coach says loudly. "You've got your schedule. Make sure you follow it." He switches the microphone from one hand to the other. "Also, curfew is at ten o'clock. You need to be in your rooms with your lights out by ten thirty."

Angela leans back on the bleachers and I copy her.

"Tomorrow morning we'll split up the boys and girls and do some skills testing. That will give us a better idea of your abilities. In the afternoon, we'll separate you into three different levels."

I sit up. What if I'm not good enough to be in the same group with Isaac, Diego, and Gig? What if we get split up?

Before we get into bed, Gig opens the window to cool down the room. The fresh smell of pine trees spills in and a stream of moonlight shines on the floor. Outside, crickets chirp up a storm.

"I'm wiped out." Gig gazes up at the ceiling.

"Me, too." Though I'm not sure how I'm going to fall asleep with all these weird noises.

"I hope that Diego's cousin doesn't try to hang out with us all the time," Gig says.

"Why?"

"I don't need to listen to some girl going on and on about how great soccer is and how a goal is the greatest thing in the world."

"She won't practice with us. She'll be with the girls."

"Yeah, but I don't want her following us around all the time. There are things you can't do if girls are around."

"Like what?"

"Like this." Gig lifts his butt and rips a machine-gun fart. The scent of pine trees disappears.

"You shouldn't have gone back for thirds." I cover my

nose with my hand. "Before that, I was glad you changed your mind and came to camp."

"Now you're not sure." Gig laughs.

"No, I wouldn't want to room by myself." We both go quiet and listen to the crickets. I think about Mom and Quinn and where we're going to live. I think about G-Man and Dad.

In the distance, a dog barks.

Gig's snoring from his side of the room. I hate how quickly he falls asleep. Now I'm left alone listening to night noises and worrying about tryouts tomorrow.

CHAPTER 7

The field is crowded with boys of different sizes kicking soccer balls. One guy with big curly hair is shifting his head and neck as he balances the ball on top of his head.

"Show-off," Gig mutters as we walk past.

"Big deal," Isaac says.

Tall pines edge the field and sun filters through them. I bend down to tie the laces on my cleats tighter. I wish we didn't have tryouts. The coaches will examine us like we're bugs under a microscope.

Gig passes me his tube of sunscreen. "Want some of this?"

"Yeah." I squeeze some out and spread it on my arms, legs, neck, and face.

Isaac turns to Diego. "What will we do in tryouts?"

"I don't know exactly." He shrugs.

"You're the one who made us sign up for this dumb camp," Gig says.

"Time out." I step forward. "We all agreed."

"What's wrong with him?" Diego points at Gig, who's walking away.

"I don't know. Maybe it's too early in the morning. He likes to sleep late in the summer."

"I do, too," Isaac says, "but I don't get bent out of shape if I don't get my way."

A whistle pierces long and sharp. "Everybody over here," Coach Derek calls.

We walk over to the sideline with everybody else.

"For the skills tests, we'll split you up in small groups and run you through a series of drills." Coach moves over to a table. "Everybody take one of these numbers stacked here. Pin it to the front of your shirt."

We line up and when my turn comes, I take number thirty-five. I carefully pin the number to my gray Under Armour shirt. Gig's struggling with his pins. "Hey, your number is upside down."

"What difference does it make?" Gig snaps the pin shut. "Like I care what level I'm on."

"Remember, the skills test is only for us to assess your ability," Coach says. "Do the best you can. Relax and have fun."

Yeah, have fun while coaches watch every move, waiting to see if you screw up.

"You six will be in a group." Coach motions the four of us and two short guys to the side.

"What grade are you in?" asks the one with his hair cut like someone put a bowl on top of his head.

"Fifth," I say.

"We're going to be in fifth, too," the one with a scar on his chin says.

"I'm not going to be in fifth," I correct. "I'm going to be in sixth. Middle school."

"You should have said that the first time." He shakes his head like I'm an idiot.

Sixth. Sixth. Sixth. I've got to get used to saying *sixth*.

"Warm up with some toe taps." Coach demonstrates on a ball in front of him.

I hop up and down and touch the ball like everybody else. I'm glad Dad showed me these in advance.

"Good." Coach blows his whistle. "Now do half scissors." He swings his leg over the ball and back.

I try to follow but hop around awkwardly. Next to me, Diego moves gracefully and Gig and Isaac pick it up, too.

"Now, full scissors." Coach swings one leg around the ball and then the other.

My legs feel like they're going in different directions and I stagger around clumsily.

Coach blows the whistle again. "Line up single file in your groups on the sideline. Dribble the ball around the orange cones."

"That's easy," says Diego.

"Yeah, for you," Isaac says.

The bowl-cut kid goes first and keeps the ball close to him. He races back and taps it to his friend. Scarface is even faster. He zips around the cones like he was born with the ball attached to his feet.

"Your turn." I push Diego forward. "Show them how it's done."

Diego taps the ball with his right foot and glides around the first cone. He darts among the cones without looking at the ball.

"I don't know if I've told you," Gig says, "but I hate soccer."

"Yeah, you mentioned that."

Isaac controls the ball as he takes wide turns around the cones.

"Use your outside foot to guide it," Diego says.

"I know what I want to do, but my feet aren't cooperating." Isaac taps the ball to me.

With my right foot, I kick the ball toward the first cone and race to catch up with it.

"Not so hard," Diego calls.

The ball rolls past the cone so I have to stop it and kick it back to get it on track. On the course beside me, a little kid is flying through. I move like an old grandpa compared to him.

On the sideline, Coach marks something down on his clipboard. "Slow down," he says. "Don't get ahead of yourself."

I focus on the ball and make the turn around the last cone and start back. How am I going to play in a game if I'm this slow and I have to look down all the time to see what I'm doing?

"Your turn." I guide the ball to Gig, who's smirking. "It's harder than it looks."

"You'll get better with practice." Diego stands beside me.

Gig races around the cones. He's fast so his speed helps him here.

"He's not bad," Diego says.

"Especially after all his whining," I add.

"Yeah." Isaac looks at me. "He's better than us. We should be the ones complaining."

I'm starved after three hours of skills testing.

"Do you think we'll all be on the same level?" Isaac says as we sit at the same table that we did last night.

"I doubt it." I chug my root beer. "I was terrible."

"Same here," he says.

On the far side of the Dining Center by the back wall, Angela sits with a bunch of girls.

I turn to Gig. "Did you say something to her?"

"Who?"

"Angela."

"Yeah. I told her to clear out—that we had some boy stuff to talk over." Gig wipes his mouth with his hand.

Angela laughs with the girls at her table. Her smile flashes all the way across the room. Maybe she'll never eat with us again.

"Let's check out the beach after lunch," Isaac says.

"Yeah." Diego digs into his meat loaf.

"Just to look," Gig says. "I'm not going in."

"We don't have time to swim now," Isaac says.

"When do we have to be back on the field?" I glance up at the clock.

"Two," Diego says.

Forty-five minutes and I don't feel like looking at the beach. "I've got to find something in my room."

"What?" Isaac asks.

"My phone charger. I don't know if I brought it." I look over at Angela's table.

What's *she* going to do?

CHAPTER 8

Angela's on the field with seven other girls in a fast-paced game of four-on-four. I stand halfway up the hill behind a tree and watch her chase a ball in the corner. She controls it and boots a pass to a teammate in the middle.

She rushes toward the goal, and the teammate sends the pass back. Angela swings her right leg forward and the ball explodes off her foot and snaps into the back of the net.

Teammates swarm around her, and Angela beams as they jog back upfield. She doesn't wave her arms above her head and jump around like scoring a goal is a huge deal. She acts like someone who's used to putting the ball in the net.

I take a step away from the tree for a better view and keep my eyes on her even when she isn't near the ball. My phone charger is safe in my bag, but I needed an excuse. I don't usually lie to my friends, especially about a girl, but Angela seems so different from ordinary girls.

Her ponytail waves back and forth as she moves confidently. Her teammates look for her because she's the best player on the field, but she passes it back and includes everybody even though she's clearly the star.

"Can I help you?"

I jump about a foot in the air. I turn around to see Lauren staring at me.

"No. No. I . . . I was looking for something behind this, this tree."

"What exactly were you looking for?" she asks.

"Ahhh, my sweatshirt." I say the first thing that pops into my mind. "I lost my sweatshirt."

"Well, it's much more likely to be down by the bench than up here," Lauren says firmly. "I'll escort you down and we'll take a look."

"No, that's okay. Maybe I left it in my room." I turn and hurry up the hill.

"Good luck finding it," Lauren calls.

She doesn't believe my lame sweatshirt story one bit.

———

At afternoon practice, Isaac, Diego, Gig, and I sit together on the grass. I lie back and the sunlight bathes my face. I close my eyes and the image I see is Angela chasing the ball.

Coach Derek blows his whistle. "We've got three different levels that we'll put you in: Universe, Galaxy, and Cosmos."

I sit up to listen.

"Level Three—Team Universe," Coach calls out, and starts reading names I don't know. He pauses before the last one. "Diego Jimenez."

"Way to go, Diego." Isaac holds out his fist and Diego pounds it.

"Thanks." Diego adjusts his shin guards under his socks.

I listen as Coach calls the names for Level Two, even though I doubt I'll be called.

"Spencer Milroy," Coach says.

"It's Gig, not Spencer," Gig shouts out.

"Either way," Coach says. "You're on Team Galaxy."

As Coach goes through the rest of the Team Galaxy names, I hope he doesn't call Isaac. I don't want to be stuck on Level One by myself.

"And the final player on Team Galaxy is"—Coach pauses to build up suspense—"Adam Waldman."

"Yeah." A red-haired kid punches his fist forward.

Isaac turns to me. "At least we're together."

"Yeah." Maybe he was thinking the same thing I was while the names were being called.

Coach reads the names of the Team Cosmos players, which is really stupid. We already know. If your name wasn't called off for one of the good teams, you're stuck at Level One.

"I'd rather be with you." Gig stands up with Isaac and me. "I don't know anybody on my team."

"Me neither." Diego pulls himself up.

"Quit trying to make us feel better for being at the lowest level," I say.

To start the practice, Coach Steve, the college student who's leading the Cosmos, splits us into two teams. Isaac and I stand so close together we look like we're attached to make sure we get on the same team. We both pull the yellow mesh tops that Coach calls pinnies over our heads. We both take positions on defense, as the smaller boys on our team run to play offense.

When Coach blows the whistle, players race around the field. I get my feet tangled up with the smallest boy and offer him a hand.

"How old are you?" I ask.

"Ten." He refuses my hand and rushes after the ball.

He doesn't look ten. I adjust the pinnie, which feels like a bib. Isaac and I are playing with kids who are a whole year younger than we are.

After practice, we all head down the hill to the lake. After four hours of running around the soccer field, I'm ready to cool off.

"How'd you do?" Isaac asks Gig.

"I had two goals." Gig wraps a towel around him like Superman's cape.

I jog to keep up. "That's pretty good for someone who hates soccer."

"Diego's right." Gig raises his arms like he's flying. "Soccer's about speed. I beat guys to the ball and kick it in."

"With some coaching, you could be good," Diego says.

"Soccer and football are the same season," Gig says. "I wouldn't give up football for anything."

Loads of people are in the water as we get to the beach. We lay out our towels and peel off our shirts. On the other side of the lake, the spire of a small chapel rises above the trees.

"Ready, set, go," Gig says. We all run and dive into the cool water.

I come up beside Gig and shake my head like a dog.

"Knock it off." He punches me in the arm.

"I thought you weren't going in any lakes because of fish poop."

"This lake looks clean, and I don't see any fish." Gig reaches over and tries to push me, but I swim away. Isaac and Diego sneak up on Gig from behind and dunk him.

Gig sputters up. "You'll pay!" He swims after them as they cut through the water to the dock.

I turn around and see Angela. She's moving up and down with smooth, strong breaststrokes. She surfaces, takes a breath, and cuts sharply down through the water.

I swim over to the side and position myself in her path. I've never met anyone like her. Angela stops a few feet from me.

"Hi." I rub my wet hair down and hope my ears don't look too big. Why can't I think of anything interesting to say?

"Oh, hi. Doesn't this feel great?" She stands before me in her bright yellow bikini, which looks great against her brown body.

"Yeah." I scrunch my toes in the sand and try to focus on her big eyes. I wonder if she thinks about me the way I think about her.

She's like an angel, like the first part of her name.

Angela.

CHAPTER 9

"**H**ey, Lover Boy, get over here," Gig hollers from the dock.

People turn to look and I'm embarrassed.

"You can talk to your girlfriend later."

"See you," I mumble to Angela, and swim toward the dock. Why can't Gig keep his fat mouth shut?

At the dock, I push myself up to climb on.

"What were you doing?" Diego raises his eyebrows.

"Falling in looooooove," Isaac answers.

"Oh, Angela. You're so beautiful," Gig says in a high-pitched voice. "I dream about you all the time."

"Shut up." I give him a shove.

"Angela." He puckers his lips and makes kissing sounds.

"Knock it off." I push harder and he slips off the dock and falls in the water.

"She's my cousin, dude." Diego shoves me from behind.

I belly flop in next to Gig, who opens his arms like he's about to hug me. "Oh, Angela."

"Shut up, Gig!" I try to sound tough as I swim away from him.

"Angela. Angela," he calls after me.

"There's fish in this lake," I yell. "I just felt one swim by."

"Really?" Gig's eyes widen.

"Yeah, hundreds of them."

Gig looks down at the water and finally shuts up.

I climb up on the dock again. Diego's talking to a guy who's even bigger than he is. Isaac's in the water talking to the blond-haired girl who said hi yesterday. I casually scan the swimmers for that yellow bikini.

There she is, swimming fast. Angela's arms slice through the water on her front crawl.

She's a strong swimmer, too.

Then out of the corner of my eye, I notice Diego's stopped talking and is watching me. I'm just admiring his cousin's swimming. There's nothing wrong with that.

At dinner, Diego introduces us to Carlos, the boy he was talking to on the dock.

"Hey, Carlos," I say.

"Carlos and I played defense together this afternoon." Diego motions for him to join our table.

"Isaac and I played defense together, too." I take my plate and silverware off my tray. "Only we didn't stop anybody."

"We'll do better tonight," Isaac says.

"What time's the next session?" Gig stuffs some bread with peanut butter into his mouth.

"Seven," Diego says.

"Oh, great," I say sarcastically.

Isaac peels a banana. "It is a soccer camp."

"I know." I spoon up cottage cheese and applesauce. "Morning, afternoon, evening—it's too much soccer."

"You're the one who begged me to come here," Gig says.

"Yeah, but I thought we'd have more time to explore."

"Explore what?" Isaac asks.

"Angela." Gig grins.

"Shut up already." At the end of the table, Diego and Carlos argue about whether Arsenal or Manchester United will win the Premier League this year. I'm glad Diego didn't hear that.

I take a bite of strawberry pie and look around the dining room. The brick walls make it feel old. Without saying anything, we've sat at this same table by the window for every meal.

I look out the window at the other old buildings on campus. I'd really rather go exploring than play more soccer.

The whole idea of coming with Diego was to stick together. Now, other than Isaac and me, we're not even on the same team.

At evening practice, Coach Steve directs Isaac and me to defense again. He throws the ball out and everybody races toward it.

I run up to midfield when the ball goes down to the other end and move around like I know what I'm doing. I thought the purpose of soccer camp was to teach you to be a better player, not just run up and down the field and try to kick the ball. It would be like going to baseball camp and playing games all the time. The players who were good would dominate and the other players would feel like they weren't getting better.

In baseball, basketball, and football, I've always been pretty good. I never paid much attention to the kids who weren't. Now I'm one of them.

A spinning ball comes my way. It takes an awkward bounce and is about to go over my shoulder. Instinctively, I stick my hand out to stop it.

"HAND BALL! HAND BALL!" everybody yells at once.

"You can't use your hand." The guy with the bowl haircut scowls at me.

I turn away. Like I don't know that. I walk over by Isaac as the other team lines up for a direct kick. A mosquito buzzes my ear, and I wave it away.

"I hate defense," I say. "It feels like everything is coming at me way too fast."

"Me, too," he says. We line up in a wall and put our hands down in front of us like our teammates do. The last thing anyone wants is a ball in the cookies. A mosquito lands on my cheek and I try to blow it off since I can't move my hands.

The scar-faced kid blasts a shot and I have to do everything I can to resist putting my hands out to block the ball. The ball zooms in and bounces off my shoulder. Everybody chases after it, and someone from the other team kicks it out of bounds.

I retrieve it and raise my hands to throw it in. I look for Isaac, but he's tightly covered. Everybody else is covered, too.

"Throw it in," Bowl Cut yells angrily.

I slap at another mosquito. This one on my forehead.

"Hurry up."

I throw the ball in and someone steals it.

"What are you doing?" Bowl Cut yells. "Throw it to our team, not their team. Don't you know anything?"

I run back toward our goal and try to stay in front of Scarface. He fakes to the inside and I take a long stride to stop him. He pivots the other way and when I try to turn, my leg is out too far and I fall back on my butt.

"You smoked him," the littlest kid taunts.

I turn to see Scarface launch a shot that catches the inside of the net.

"GOOOOOAL!" he hollers, and raises his arms.

"Mark your man!" Bowl Cut yells.

I slap another mosquito and wipe the blood from my arm. This game is too hard.

CHAPTER 10

"**I**saac and I are together." I run over to the far side of the foosball table that's in the basement of our dorm.

"Really?" Gig says. "Diego and I will kick your butts."

"It's foosball, not soccer." Isaac spins his men.

"Do you want front or back?" I turn to Isaac.

"I'm better up front," he says.

I spin the handles of the two defensemen and the goalie of the red team. "Look, they don't have arms. There's no way I'll get called for a hand ball."

Isaac picks up a white ball from the tray and holds it at the chute. "Ready?"

"Let it roll," Diego says.

Isaac lets go and Gig cranks his players. The white ball cracks off the side and Gig swings to shoot. I slide my man over to block his shot and the ball scoots forward to Isaac. He winds up and fires a goal.

"Great shot!" I shout.

"One to nothing," Isaac calls.

"Lucky shot," Diego sneers.

Isaac blows on his hand. "Not lucky at all." He picks up the ball and drops it down.

Handles fly and the ball ricochets around the table. Gig passes it from the side, but I anticipate his shot and block it again. Isaac banks a pass off the board and blasts a shot that bangs wide.

Diego controls the rebound and launches a shot up the middle that goes through everyone but smacks against my goalie. Complete luck on the stop. Sometimes, though, luck is better than skill.

Isaac passes to the middle and kicks a roller that beats Diego's goalie.

"Two to nothing!" I holler.

"We're destroying you," Isaac adds.

We blast the ball around the table and I get to release all of my frustrations from the soccer field on these plastic red men and the white ball.

Finally something Isaac and I are good at.

At lights-out, I climb into my bed and lie on my back. I don't feel tired at all after our foosball triumph. I'm all jazzed up.

"I can't believe you beat us." Gig bounces on his bed.

"We won three games in a row."

"You cheated on the last game."

"How?"

"Isaac rolled the ball before I was ready," Gig says. "I called time-out."

"You can't call time-out in the middle of foosball."

"Yes, you can. Anyway, it was beginner's luck. We'll cream you tomorrow."

"We'll see." I roll over on my side. "How was your evening practice?"

"Okay," Gig says. "I had a goal, but Adam Waldman and some of the other guys on my team are too hard-core. They act like soccer is life or death."

Life or death. Gig's dad is getting ready to go someplace that really is life or death. "Yeah, some of my teammates are like that, too."

"I wish I was playing with you and Isaac," Gig says.

"I do, too, but you're doing good at Level Two."

"It's a lot more fun with friends."

Gig's deep asleep on the other side of the room.

I can't sleep.

The light from the moon seems too bright.

I can't sleep.

I scratch the mosquito bites on my arm, cheek, and forehead.

I can't sleep.

Tap, tap, tap.

I sit up and listen. Somebody's at the door.

"Jackson, Gig." *Tap, tap.*

I scramble out of bed and open the door. Isaac, who's dressed, puts a finger to his lips. I wave for him to come inside.

"What are you doing?"

"I'm wide awake," he says.

"Me, too. I'm buzzing about smashing them in foosball."

"Yeah, and it's a full moon. It's so bright out."

"Huh?" Gig stirs in his sleep. "No. Go."

"What did he say?"

I shrug. "I don't know. He talks in his sleep sometimes."

"Let's go out," Isaac says.

"We can't. We're not supposed to leave the dorm after ten."

"Who's going to know?" Isaac says. "And you're the one who said you wanted to explore. Let's go."

I look over at Gig, who's snoring again.

"Is he always that loud?" Isaac asks.

"Usually."

"Grab some clothes. Come on."

I throw on shorts, a T-shirt, and sandals. "Wait, I've got an idea." I pull out other clothes and stuff them under the blankets of my bed. "In case Gig wakes up."

"Good plan." Isaac slowly twists the knob of the door and peeks out. He waves me forward and together we tiptoe down the hall like escaping prisoners.

As we turn the corner and come up to Room 324, Isaac points. The paper sign in the shape of a soccer ball reads:

COACH DEREK

CAMP DIRECTOR

We pass silently and continue down the hall. I hold the door while it slowly closes so it won't make a noise.

Outside, we start up the hill and I hurry to keep up with Isaac.

"Where are we going?" I whisper.

"Exploring," Isaac says. "We'll start with the place on campus you want to see the most."

"What?"

"You know."

"What?"

"The girls' dorm," Isaac says.

I smile. "How'd you know?"

"I saw you at the lake today." Isaac keeps up the fast pace. Ahead of us is an old gray building that looks like a castle. "That's it."

"Are you sure?" We walk closer.

"I looked at the map they gave us and asked Crystal, the girl I was talking to at the lake."

We stand and stare. All the lights are out in the rooms, but I try to guess which one is Angela's. I pick one and imagine her and what she's wearing. Maybe she can't sleep, either. Maybe she's standing at the window looking out at us.

"Listen," Isaac says.

I hear someone coming down the walk.

"Quick." Isaac waves and I follow him behind some bushes. My heart's thumping so hard I'm afraid we'll be caught. I bend down to make myself smaller and watch the path. The footsteps come closer and a woman walks under a light. She stops and looks around like she's heard something. Neither Isaac nor I move a muscle even though a mosquito buzzes around my face.

She walks toward the dorm and just before she opens the door, she takes one more look around.

"Let's get out of here." I run down the sidewalk.

"No, over here." Isaac pulls me out from under the lights and we run across the grass. We run and run and don't stop until we're down by the lake.

"Who was it?" Isaac says.

"Lauren." I struggle to catch my breath.

"Who?"

"Lauren, the girls' coach." I kick off my sandals and dip my toes in the cold water. I don't need to be caught by her for the second time today. She might kick me out of camp.

"There's supposed to be a path down here that goes out to the chapel," Isaac says. "Let's find it."

"I don't know." I look around but feel like somebody's watching us. "I don't want to get caught."

"Nobody's going to be looking for us down here." Isaac searches through trees. "I've found it."

The lake looks smooth as a mirror.

"C'mon," Isaac says.

"I'm getting bit up out here."

"Didn't you use bug spray?"

"No."

"You've got to use that up here." Isaac starts ahead. "Come on. We'll just go a little way."

I slip into my sandals and hurry to catch up on the gravel path. The light of the moon casts long shadows that form spooky shapes.

"We need a light," I whisper.

"We can see okay." Isaac pushes ahead of me.

I hesitate at a narrow section where the gravel ends. We both are so quiet I can hear my breathing.

We follow the path up a hill and then down by the lake.

"I'm ready to go back." I turn around.

"Just a little farther." Isaac pushes me forward.

I step on a pinecone that crackles in the stillness, and I stop dead in my tracks.

Ahead, at the edge of the lake, a long dark shape floats above the water. It's bigger than us and it's coming straight toward us.

"Run!" I turn to Isaac. "Fast!"

CHAPTER 11

Back in front of our dorm, I bend down with my hands on my knees.

"I didn't see it," Isaac gasps. "What was it?"

"Something black. Floating toward us. It looked like . . . like . . . a ghost."

"No way. It wasn't a ghost." Isaac shakes his head.

"That's exactly what it looked like."

"You're seeing things."

"Yeah, a ghost."

Isaac slides his key card, waits for the green signal, and opens the door. We creep up the stairs quietly. The last thing we need is to get busted sneaking back to our rooms after curfew.

While Isaac goes to his room, I go to mine. I try to be as silent as possible as I open the door and move inside. I close it gently and hear the click.

I turn around and just about jump out of my skin. Gig's sitting up on his bed staring at me. "Where have you been?"

"Out exploring. With Isaac," I whisper. "You almost scared me to death."

"Why wasn't I with you?"

"Gig, you were sound asleep."

He gets up and walks toward me. "You should have woken me up. Where did you go?"

"The lake."

"What happened? You look weird."

"I saw something." My hands are still shaking so I sit down on my bed and press them against my thighs.

"What?"

"Promise you won't think I'm crazy."

"What did you see?"

"We were walking along this path and something came directly at us. A ghost. A black ghost."

"You're crazy," Gig says. "At Longview on the school visit, you said you saw a white ghost. Now you say you saw a black ghost. What's next? A green ghost?"

"You promised."

"Promised what?"

"That you wouldn't think I was crazy."

"Well, it is crazy," Gig says. "I won't believe it unless I see that ghost myself."

I pull off my shorts and T-shirt.

"Don't do this stupid stuffed-clothes-in-your-bed trick, either." Gig throws the clothes at me. "I thought you were dead when I didn't see you breathing."

"Sorry."

"And don't go without me next time. Got it?"

"Okay, okay. I promise."

At practice the next morning, I'm tired before we've even started. I sit next to Isaac on the bench and scratch my bug bites.

He yawns. "I want to go back to bed."

"Me, too." The yawn's contagious. "I couldn't sleep after we got back. I kept tossing and turning and thinking about the ghost."

"It wasn't a ghost."

"Yes, it was."

"This morning we'll focus on skill development," Coach Steve says in his cheery voice that bugs me already.

Across the field, Gig's sitting with the other players in Team Galaxy and Diego's with the stars from Team Universe.

Coach frowns. "Yesterday, some of the technique was sloppy. We need to improve to a level we can be proud of."

I stare over at the far field where the girls are practicing and make out Angela. What would she say if I told her about the ghost? I bet she wouldn't doubt me or say I was crazy.

Coach blows his whistle. "Let's go."

I shuffle out with Isaac.

"We're the only sixth graders in this group," he says.

"How do you know?"

"I asked. We're the only sixth graders who got sent down a level."

"Form a line facing me," Coach says.

Isaac and I grab spots at the end.

"I'll pass the ball to the first person," Coach says, "and then you go one-on-one against Brady, the goalie." He points over his shoulder. "Make a move and drill the ball into the back of the net."

Brady, in the neon-green goalie jersey, paces back and forth between the posts as he tightens the Velcro on his gloves. He stretches out his arms and rolls them around in circles.

"Here we go." Coach kicks the ball to Bowl Cut.

He runs forward, fakes a shot, and then moves to the center. Brady stays down in his crouch and slides to his left to block the angle. Bowl Cut fires and buries the goal just inside the near post.

"Good." Coach kicks a pass to Scarface. "Next."

He blasts a quick shot trying to catch Brady off guard, but he sees it coming and hugs the ball to his chest.

"Good stop." Coach claps.

When Isaac's turn comes, he dribbles the ball and tries to fake a shot, but he can't control it and the ball gets away from him and rolls harmlessly past the end line.

"Next up." Coach taps me a ball.

I jog in looking at the ball. Don't try anything too fancy, I tell myself.

"Head up, Kennedy," Coach shouts. "Eyes on the goal."

I kick the ball but don't get much on it, and Brady makes an easy save.

"Do something with the ball," Coach says. "Have an idea what you want to do."

I jog back to the end of the line. Last night I wished we could have more instruction on how to play. Now that we have it, I'd rather just run around and play a game.

When it comes to soccer, I don't know what I want.

CHAPTER 12

After lunch I fill my glass with root beer at the beverage station and watch Angela talking to Carlos and a group of her friends. I take a gulp and wish I was at that table.

But other than Angela, I don't know any of them. I press the root beer button again to top off my drink.

"See you in a little bit." Angela waves good-bye to the girls and they split up. She follows Carlos over to the dessert bar, where he swirls a mixture of chocolate and strawberry ice cream into a cup. He leans toward her and says something and she laughs. Are the two of them friends?

I finish my drink, and even though I'm not thirsty anymore, press the root beer button again.

"See you later," Angela says to Carlos.

"Later." Carlos spoons up a scoop of ice cream.

I set my glass down and follow her through the wooden doors and then out the glass doors to the outside.

"Hey, Angela." I try to sound like I just saw her.

"Oh, hi."

"Where are you going?" I rub the mosquito bite on my cheek that feels the size of a grape. I hope she doesn't think it's a giant zit.

"Down to the field to work on corner kicks."

"Do you need someone to practice with?"

"No." She shakes her head. "I'm meeting a friend."

"Okay." I look down at the crack that splits the concrete.

"See you around." She waves and walks away.

I turn around toward my dorm. I wanted to tell her about the ghost and see what she'd say. I just wanted to talk to her.

I wipe sweat from my face with my blue shirt. There's not a cloud in the sky and the sun beats down. It must be in the high nineties. I'm glad Dad got me these new shirts.

Coach splits the Cosmos into two teams and Isaac's playing forward on the other one while I'm stuck on defense.

The whistle blows and the opponents rush toward us. The ball's kicked to the center and I stick my foot out to break up the pass. I control the ball and pass back to Brady, the goalie, who comes forward.

"Nice play," he says.

I run downfield as we advance the ball. A steal on the other end results in a high kick. I position myself under it like I'm catching a pop fly in baseball. Instead of my hands, I bump the ball with my forehead like we worked on in skills practice this morning.

"That's the way, Kennedy," Coach calls. "Now you're using your head."

Isaac breaks free on a rush and I run over to cut him off. He reverses directions and I slide past. I hop up and chase after him. He passes the ball and sprints to the middle. I stay with him and stick my foot out to break up the pass coming back to him. He bumps into me and I fall to the ground. I look up, expecting a penalty call from Coach, but there's nothing. I don't understand what's a penalty in this game and what isn't.

I jump up and chase after the play. The ball skids wide and I race Isaac to it. We arrive at the same time and swing our legs to kick. I get all ball, but Isaac kicks my knee. I fall backward and grab it.

Again, no whistle.

I get up and take my position. I'm sure Isaac didn't mean to kick me, but it hurts all the same.

I fall back on defense, and Isaac and Bowl Cut race toward me. Isaac passes and rushes to the center. Bowl Cut passes a ball that's above my head. Without thinking, I raise my hand to stop it.

"HAND BALL! HAND BALL!" everybody shouts.

I kick the ground. My second hand ball in two days. I want to hide. I can't help myself. Every sport I play, I use my hands. It's impossible to keep them by my side.

Bowl Cut takes control on the free kick and blasts a goal. Brady looks over at me with disgust, and I bend over with my hands on my knees so I don't have to look at any of my teammates.

After practice I can't wait to get to the lake. Partly because it's so hot and I want to cool off. Partly to wash away the embarrassment of another hand ball. But mainly to see if Angela's there in her yellow bikini.

"How'd your game go, Ghost Hunter?" Gig asks as we cut across campus.

"I had another hand ball. I can't stop using my hands."

"Another one? Maybe we should duct tape them to your side. That would stop it."

"That might be the only way." I hurry to keep up with him. "How'd you do?"

"Two goals. Easy ones. The ball was passed to me and the goalie was out of position. I just knocked the ball in."

"Awesome." We move down the hill.

"The game isn't hard. You just kick it where they aren't."

"It's hard for me."

"Hey, I've got an idea." Gig turns to me.

"What?"

"You're in the wrong position."

"What do you mean?"

"You shouldn't be playing defense."

"I know. I hate it."

"You should play offense like I do. You won't be so tempted to use your hands."

"You think so?" I scan the swimmers at the beach looking for Angela.

"Yeah."

I look for a yellow bikini in the water, but can't find one. Maybe she's wearing a different suit today.

"Come on," Gig yells. "What are you waiting for?"

I chase after him and we dive into the lake together. The cool water feels so good that I stay under as long as I can. Sometimes I think it would be great to be a fish and never have to come up for air.

When I finally surface I look around. Then I spot *her*. She is wearing her yellow bikini. She's lying back on the beach with a towel spread out under her. And sitting right next to her, with his towel touching hers, is Carlos.

I feel like I've stepped off a drop-off and am thrashing around underwater. I've been such an idiot. He's a soccer star. I'm a nobody. Of course she wants to hang out with a big soccer star.

CHAPTER 13

After dinner, we resume our foosball challenge.

"No good." I hold up my hands.

"That goal so counts," Gig says.

"I wasn't ready."

"Too bad, so sad." Diego grins.

I turn to Isaac. "Wait until I'm ready."

"Well, get ready," he snaps. "Pay attention."

"I am." I spin my men back and forth. Isaac's right, though. I wasn't focused on foosball. I was thinking about something else: Angela and Carlos.

"Are you ready now?" Isaac holds the ball directly in front of my nose.

"Yes!" I snap.

The ball rolls onto the table, and Isaac flicks a pass forward. He fires a shot, but it bounces hard off the side. The rebound kicks all the way to the middle of the table where Diego blasts a shot. It's in before I even move my goalie.

"Focus," Isaac says.

"I didn't have a chance."

"Let me play defense." Isaac slides over. "You go up front."

"Fine." I grab the front bars. "You wouldn't have stopped that, either."

"Six, zip," Gig says. "We own you."

I check to see that Isaac's ready and roll the ball out. Diego taps the ball forward and slides his men and shoots. Isaac moves his defender and blocks the shot.

I pass forward and try to control it with my man, but the ball skips off. My hands can't keep up with what my brain wants them to do. Gig's guy banks a pass to Diego. He cranks up and blasts another winner.

"Seven, zip," Gig shouts.

Isaac glares at me.

I slam the bars against the table. I can't do anything right today.

I can't sleep again. I roll around trying to find a comfortable position on the hard mattress. What a lousy day. Bad soccer, bad foosball, and Angela and Carlos together. Why did I think I had a chance with her anyway?

I get out of bed and walk to the window by Gig's bed, where he snores away. Outside the moonlight shines brightly.

"Gig, Gig." I shake his shoulder.

He turns over but keeps snoring.

"Gig." I press harder.

"Unn." He stirs.

"Gig. Get up." I shake him in the back.

"What? What's up?"

"I'm going exploring."

"Now?"

"No, in three days," I say sarcastically. "Yes, now. Get up."

I go to my closet and put on jeans and a sweatshirt. Gig gets dressed, too, without saying anything. I remember the bug spray and cover my face, neck, and ears. The mosquitoes will smell me coming from a mile away.

"Here, use some of this." I toss it to Gig. I sit down on the edge of my bed and put on my socks and Nikes. I can run better in shoes if I need to. I grab my baseball hat and put it on.

I put my finger to my lips as I open the door and look both ways. We both tiptoe down the tiled hall.

When we get outside, Gig turns to me. "Where are we going?"

"The lake," I whisper as we walk through campus. I point out the old gray building. "That's the girls' dorm."

"Let's go there," Gig says.

"No." I shake my head. "We're on a mission."

"What mission?"

"Follow me." I walk faster past the old brick buildings and down the hill. Below us the moon reflects on the surface of the lake, and the water gently laps at the shore. It's so quiet now compared to the afternoon noise of the swimmers and divers that it doesn't feel like the same place.

"Over here." I find the gravel path between the trees.

"Where are we going?" Gig asks.

"The path to the chapel. It goes along the edge of the lake."

Gig follows behind me. Normally he's the one getting me to do things so it feels kind of cool to take charge. I move a branch to the side in case we've got to run back. We walk around the curve and up the hill that I remember from last night. Somehow with Gig here, the shadows don't seem quite so scary.

"Here's the spot." I stop.

"What spot?"

"Where Isaac and I saw it. You know . . . the black ghost."

"Where?"

I point down to the lake's edge. "Right there."

Gig peers down and I do, too. Nothing's moving.

"It wasn't a ghost," Gig says.

"What was it, then?"

"Who ever heard of a black ghost?" Gig says.

"That's what makes it even scarier. It's not an ordinary ghost."

Gig steps over a tree root and I hurry to catch up. At least he's not saying I'm crazy anymore.

"Show me exactly where it was," Gig says.

"Down here." I climb over branches as I move to the edge of the lake. I bend down to look closely.

Gig bends down, too. "No footprints, no tracks. Nothing."

"Just like a ghost." I nod.

"That doesn't prove anything." Gig looks around cautiously.

"It might." I take a couple more steps. "Let's go a little farther."

"Why?" Gig asks.

"To see where the path goes." I brush against ferns as I follow the path along the lake. I take longer strides as we climb up a hill that has a big rock beside the trail.

"See, there's nothing out here." Gig stops at the top.

"Let's just go a little bit more." Ahead of us the chapel stands on a point that sticks out into the lake.

We step carefully along the path that cuts through a stand of tall pine trees. I look up at the straight trunks that climb into the night sky. A cloud floats across the moon, and suddenly, it's dark.

Gig trips against me and I grab hold of him.

"Listen," he whispers. "I heard something."

Neither one of us moves as a light breeze ripples the lake. The cloud floats past and the moonlight shines down. I take one step forward and Gig grabs my arm.

Below us, two black shapes stand at the edge of the lake.

Gig grabs me tight and we're frozen in place. We're deep in the woods with two ghosts. Gig lets go of me and staggers backward.

All of the sudden, both ghosts turn toward us.

"Run," I say, but Gig's already flying down the path.

CHAPTER 14

"**W**e got"—Gig pauses for breath—"to tell." He bends over in front of our dorm. "Diego and Isaac."

"In the morning," I whisper.

"No, now."

"Shhh. Not so loud. I'm not waking them up."

"Go back to bed, then." He slides his key and opens the door and we climb the stairs. I follow after him as he opens the inside door and heads down the hall.

Then we stop. Ahead of us, a door's opening. That's Coach Derek's room. Gig jerks me by the back of my sweatshirt and pulls me into the bathroom. Steps come toward us, and Gig waves me into the showers. We scramble into the far shower and slide behind the curtain. We both squat down like that will make us less likely to be seen.

Coach shuffles to the urinal. If we get caught for being outside after curfew, we're dead meat.

I hold as still as I can and try not to breathe. When the lever's pressed to flush, I wipe my forehead and exhale. We wait a couple of minutes after Coach leaves to give him time to get back to his room.

Gig and I step lightly out of the shower, and Gig opens the door slowly to peek out. He gives me an all-clear wave and we walk as quietly as possible.

Gig goes past our room to Isaac and Diego's, and I shake my head and point back to our room. Gig nods his head vigorously up and down and I shake mine hard side to side. Then he turns and opens their door.

I've got no choice so I follow him into their room.

"We should get back to our room before Coach catches us."

"Don't worry." Gig sits down on Isaac's bed, and Isaac stirs awake.

"What's going on?" he says.

"Something freaky." Gig goes over to Diego's bed and taps him on the back. He doesn't wake up, so Gig taps harder. He doesn't wake up, so Gig sits on top of him, and Diego finally opens his eyes.

"What? What?" Diego sits up.

"Remember how Jackson said he saw a ghost when he was with you and none of us believed him?"

"Yeah." Isaac nods.

"Well, tonight we saw *two* black ghosts."

Diego's jaw drops and he stares at us like we're part of a dream.

"Two ghosts?" Isaac asks. "The same kind?"

"Identical," I say. "Twin ghosts."

"Walking on the water," Gig says.

"By the water," I say. "They were coming toward us."

"On the water," Gig insists. "They tried to capture us."

"What did you do?" Isaac asks.

"We ran back here as fast as we could," Gig says. "To get you. We should all go back out there together."

"No way," Isaac says.

Diego shakes his head no.

"Me neither, Gig." I get up. "I'm glad you saw them so you believe me, but I'm not going back into those woods."

At practice the next morning, the sky is overcast and a cool wind whips across the field. Goose bumps appear on my arms and I wish I'd worn my sweatshirt.

After two hours of drills, we're divided into teams for a short game, and again Isaac and I are split up. We're playing defense for opposing teams so we're about as far away from each other as we can get.

"Fire up!" Bowl Cut claps, trying to sound like a coach.

I rub my arms trying to warm up. Coach Steve blows his whistle and players chase after the ball. Our forwards pass it between themselves and keep the pressure on so that the ball is in their end for a long time.

Then a bouncing ball comes my way. I bump the ball down with my chest and pass it to Scarface. He loses it and I race back to mark my guy. He takes a pass and tries a fancy fake to get by me, but I hold my ground and knock the ball out of bounds.

I retreat on the throw in and hold my hands at my sides like they're tied to my body. The pass goes to Bowl Cut, who blasts a shot at our goal. Brady is slow to react and the ball gets past him.

One to zero.

We storm right back but miss two chances: one with a shot wide and another where the ball hits the post. But then Scarface boots a long shot that their goalie isn't ready for and the game is tied at one.

Coach checks his watch. "Sudden death. Next goal wins."

I retreat to my position and remind myself about using my hands. A hand ball would be the worst thing to happen now. The ball is booted to Isaac and he makes a nice spin move to free himself and kick the ball forward.

The opponents rush forward with extra energy and I check Bowl Cut on the wing. A pass flies to him and he chases it as I close in. He passes to the center and I turn to see Brady out of position again. Fortunately the shot is muffed and floats off to the side.

"Finish it off," Coach calls. "Then we can get some lunch."

I control a pass and kick it to Scarface. He dribbles up-field, but the ball is stolen. I retreat in front of the goal as players rush at me. The pass goes to the center, then to the side, then back to the center. I get turned around and stick my foot out to block the ball.

It pops up in the air, and the worst thing imaginable happens. It floats up over Brady's outstretched arm and lands in our own net.

I put my hands on my head.

"What are you doing?" Scarface yells at me.

The other team is jumping up and down in celebration.

"Two to one!"

"We win!"

Coach blows his whistle. "Defense, you need to communicate. You need to work better together."

I take off my cleats and slam them together. There is one thing worse than a hand ball—kicking the ball into your own goal.

CHAPTER 15

When I wake up from my nap, I don't know where I am. Not Mom's house. Not Dad's house. No place familiar. Beside me my phone reads 1:30, but it's not night. Then I remember I'm at soccer camp, and afternoon practice starts in half an hour. I look over at Gig's empty bed.

I'm still tired and don't feel like getting up. I've got to stop running into ghosts in the middle of the night.

I roll over to rest a few more minutes. I close my eyes and see the disaster of my own kick floating over Brady's arm in slow motion. Watching the ball land in our goal is a nightmare.

The next thing I know it's two o'clock. Time for practice. I jump out of bed, grab my gear, and race down the hall. The coaches hate anyone being late. I fly out the door and sprint down the sidewalk.

I rush past an older monk wearing a sweater and walking with a cane. No other soccer players are around. Everyone is already at practice.

I jump down the stairs three at a time and hurry across the parking lot. I rush past the tennis courts and the flower beds. I cross the road and race up the hill. I run down the gravel road under the cottonwood trees whose leaves are rattling in the wind. I jog onto the field where Coach Steve is demonstrating passing techniques with Isaac.

"Look who finally made it." He stops the drill and makes a big show about checking his watch. "Ten after two. You know what that means, Kennedy," he says sternly. "Ten laps around the entire field."

I sit down on the bench and put on my shin guards, socks, and cleats. Ten laps are going to take forever. I tie my shoes tightly and start jogging. I go past where Diego and the other stars are passing the ball with Coach Derek.

At the end of the field a couple of goalies in their neon-green jerseys are working on their footwork. The temperature has dropped and the clouds have gotten darker.

After my tenth lap, I join the practice in progress. Coach Steve makes me stand on the sideline for five more minutes to watch. He doesn't realize this isn't punishment. Nothing's going right with soccer anyway.

When I finally get in, he puts me on offense in a four-on-four drill. Bowl Cut shoots a pass that bounces off my foot.

"Control the ball," Coach calls.

A light mist begins to fall and I wish I was wearing my jacket. The ball gets booted out of bounds and I retrieve it for the throw in. Everyone on my team is covered and I don't want to make a mistake. Then I spot Isaac behind everybody else and throw the ball to him.

Coach's whistle pierces the air. "You can't do that, Kennedy. Your back foot came off the ground. You need to have both of them down. Yellow ball."

I shuffle onto the field.

"Learn the rules," Bowl Cut says.

"Shut up." The ball is thrown in and I chase after it. I plant my foot, but it slides out from under me on the wet grass. I land on my butt and everyone laughs.

I get up and try to wipe mud off my leg. What are we doing out here in the rain?

"We're going to stay out here until we connect on some of these passes," Coach warns.

The way we're going, we could be out here all night.

I pass the ball to the center and jog up the side taking short, choppy strides so I won't slip again. The center passes back, but the ball is behind me.

"Pass the ball to where the player will be," Coach corrects.

He makes us do it over and over until he decides it's acceptable.

"Listen up," he says. "Tomorrow we start our tournament. We'll place you on teams and we expect maximum effort out of each of you."

The rain is falling harder now and I'm soaked to the bone and shivering.

Tournament. Tournament. Tournament. Coach makes us stand in the rain while he goes on and on about the two-day tournament.

Who cares about the stupid tournament?

Coach finally finishes his talk. "One last announcement. The pool in the field house is open for anyone who wants to swim."

I catch up to Isaac walking off the field. "Do you want to swim?"

"No, I'm meeting Crystal." He pulls a towel from his bag and wipes his face.

I run my hand through my wet hair. He and I were the only ones on the same team, and now he's ditching me, too.

Back on the field, Gig and Diego are still practicing with their teams. I don't feel like standing around watching in the rain, so I walk over to the field house.

The building contains the indoor athletic areas and has high ceilings and concrete walls. It's not clear where the pool is. I walk down long, empty corridors before I finally find a sign. I open a heavy metal door and the smell of chlorine greets me. The pool is laid out for lap swimming, not for fun, and adults wearing swim caps fill the lanes. I don't feel like swimming at all.

I trudge back outside in the rain. Another bad day at soccer camp. I've had enough.

*B*ack in the room, my phone rings and it's Mom.

"Hey, I thought you were going to call me," she says.

"I've been really busy."

"How's soccer camp?"

"Fine." I don't feel like going into it.

"You don't sound too enthusiastic. What's the matter?"

"Nothing. We just finished a tough practice in the rain and I'm soaked. I need to take a hot shower."

"I won't keep you long, then. Quinn and I went out for ice cream last night with Ted and the girls. We had a lot of fun, but we missed you."

I pull my wet shirt off while Mom goes on about Quinn, Ted, Haley, and Heather.

"Mom," I interrupt her. "Where are we going to live next month when Liz and Jeff come back?"

"Don't worry about that. I'm looking at a couple of places this week. I'll figure something out. Besides, Ted says if we need a place for a while, we can always stay with him. He's got a big house with lots of room."

Outside, the rain's coming down harder now.

"Jackson, are you there?"

I wait a couple of seconds. "I don't want to."

"What? I lost you there for a bit."

"I don't want to move into Ted's house."

"Jackson, don't worry so much about things. I'll take care of it. You just have fun at camp."

"Yeah. Whatever."

CHAPTER 16

At dinner, Gig and I grab pieces of pizza as we go through the line. I take two glasses at the beverage station and fill them with root beer. I wait for Gig while he fills his four with a mixture of half Mountain Dew and half Dr. Pepper.

Isaac's at a table by the salad bar talking to Crystal. Diego's at a big table with the soccer stars. Angela is sitting with Carlos at *our* table, and she's giggling at one of his stupid jokes. I stand stuck in the middle, not knowing where to sit.

"Let's go in the back." Gig leads me through the dining room, past *our* table, where I don't look at either of them. I guess it's not really *our* table anymore if none of us uses it.

I sit down at a seat next to the brick wall and take a bite of the pizza. The crust is soft and doughy like it hasn't been cooked enough.

"How come you didn't wake me before practice?" I set the pizza on my plate and stare at Gig.

"My dad called from Mississippi, where he's finishing up National Guard training. I needed some time to talk."

"What did he say?"

"He wanted to know if I was having a good time."

"What did you tell him?"

"I lied." Gig folds his pizza in half and takes a bite. "He's got enough to worry about."

"I lied to my mom about it, too. At least you're doing okay. You've scored a bunch of goals."

Gig finishes his glass. "I don't like my teammates. They get jealous when I score because I'm not a 'real' soccer player."

"What does that mean?"

"I don't play in a league. I'm not going out for soccer in the fall. I don't care who plays for Chelsea or Barcelona."

"But you score goals."

"They don't like that. They think only 'real' soccer players should score. So now they freeze me out. They don't pass me the ball."

"Jerks." I shake my head. "Still, it's better than playing with a bunch of fifth graders who yell at Isaac and me every time we make a mistake."

"I hate soccer," Gig says.

"Same here." I pick sausage and cheese off my pizza. "Did your dad say anything else? About going?"

"Yeah, he's done with training in a week."

"Then what happens?"

"He goes straight to Afghanistan."

"And you don't get to see him before that?"

Gig shakes his head. "I won't see him for a whole year."

I can't imagine being separated from my dad like that.

"There's nothing I can do about it," Gig says.

After dinner, we tromp into the practice gym in the field house since it's pouring outside.

"Set your jackets by the wall," Coach Steve calls.

I take mine off and look around.

This gym is huge with enough space for three basketball courts. The floor is some kind of hard spongy material. I wish we could just forget about soccer and do something fun.

"Team Cosmos over here," Coach says.

I walk over with Isaac. "I wish we could play basketball in here."

"Me, too," he says. "Anything but soccer."

"We're going to run our dribbling drill in here." Coach lays out the orange cones. "Start in slow motion."

I go to the end of the line, and when my turn comes, I move slowly, concentrating on the ball.

"Look up," Coach calls.

I hear arguing from the next court and see Gig waving his arms at three of his teammates.

Coach claps. "Speed it up."

I move faster, and it's harder to control the ball. A couple times it comes close to getting away from me before I recover and get it back on course.

Outside, the rain whips down in sheets. There's one good thing about rain like that. Gig can't get us to go back out in the woods hunting for ghosts tonight.

"Full speed," Coach hollers. "Go as fast as you can."

I take off running, but immediately the ball skids off into the other court.

"What are you doing?" One of the stars of the Universe stops.

"Sorry." I chase after the ball.

"Hang on to your balls," he says.

I bend down to pick up my ball and get out of his way.

"Soccer, Kennedy," Coach hollers. "Don't touch the ball with your hands."

"Yeah, don't touch your balls with your hands," another star says, and everybody laughs at me.

I kick the ball against the wall and walk back to the end of the line.

At the far end of the gym, the girls are running through the same drill. Angela rushes around the cones with ease. I can't believe I was that into her. That feels like ages ago.

I scratch the bug bite on my arm and try not to think about that or where we're going to live with Mom. I've never even seen Ted's house, but I don't want to move in there and pretend we're one big happy family.

Two courts over, Diego dribbles the ball with the stars, and next to us, Gig continues to argue with his teammates. We were supposed to come up here to have fun together, but we're more split up than we've been all summer. And we're *not* having fun.

I wish I could leave right now.

CHAPTER 17

*T*hursday morning I check my cell phone. Still thirty minutes to breakfast and I'm starving. Gig's snoring like a grizzly bear.

I pull my pillow around my ears and stare up at the ceiling. The plaster pattern looks like cottage cheese suspended in place. Even that makes me hungry. The white walls of this room remind me of a hospital. It's like I'm lying on an operating table waiting for surgery.

Gig rolls over and his snoring decreases to a loud rumble. I turn over on my stomach and wrap the pillow around my head. Slowly I float into that zone between being asleep and being awake.

I see an image of myself playing soccer. I'm quick. I react. I anticipate where the ball is going to go. But best of all, I get to use my hands and no one yells at me or calls a penalty.

At breakfast, I pile my plate with pancakes, scrambled eggs, and sausage and get some orange juice. Gig and I automatically go to our new table in the back of the dining room. I butter my pancakes from the little containers, pour syrup, and dig in.

"Your snoring was terrible."

"Say what?" Gig looks up, surprised.

"Your snoring kept me awake."

"I don't snore." Gig shovels up his eggs.

"You do too."

"Nah," Gig says. "You're imagining it."

"Why would I do that?"

"I don't know." Gig grins. "Maybe you're tired of me being so perfect."

In the middle of the room, Isaac, who's by himself, looks around for a table.

"Isaac," I shout.

He sees us and comes over.

"Hey," he says.

"Hey." I move my tray to make room.

Gig looks up and belches.

"Nice." Isaac sits down. "Tournament this afternoon."

"I know. I wish we could all be on the same team."

"Me, too," Isaac says as a bunch of fifth graders pass our table acting cool like they're the kings of the college.

I stab my sausage. "I'm sure we'll be split up."

Isaac and I sit on the bench and tie our cleats. We're early, the first ones from our group. I take a deep breath. The air smells fresh after last night's rain and the sky is bright blue.

"Get in goal," Isaac says. "Let's see if you can stop me."

I go over to the goal and stand in the middle. The goal, which seems so small when you're trying to score, feels a lot bigger when you're trying to keep the ball out.

"Ready?" Isaac taps the ball between his feet.

I nod and he comes toward me. I'm not sure if I should go out or stay back. Instead I move left as he cuts to the center. He shoots a low bouncer that I drop to my knees and smother. Just like stopping one of Gig's wild pitches in baseball.

"Let me try again," Isaac says.

I roll the ball back to him.

"Ready?" he yells.

"Go." I bend down.

He approaches and fires a laser. I dive right, stick both arms out, and hang on tight.

"Lucky stop," Isaac grumbles. "I thought that was in."

"Skill." I roll the ball back to him. It's like grabbing a throw in dodgeball.

Isaac blasts a shot before I'm set and the ball slings into the net.

"Goal." He raises his arms.

"No way." I wave my arms. "I wasn't ready."

"That's your problem."

"Try one more." I throw the ball long and he chases it down.

I bend down in my crouch and shake my arms out. Isaac fakes a shot and charges toward me. He stops and boots a shot to the left, just inside the pole. I dive and punch my right hand out. I hit the ball, which sails harmlessly outside the goal.

"That would have been in," he says.

"Not with me here."

More players stream onto the field as Coach stands in the middle and puts his sunglasses on.

I take two steps toward him and stop. No, he won't listen to me.

Behind the goal, Isaac's picking up the ball and I take two steps that way.

I turn and go back in the direction of Coach. I've got nothing to lose.

"Coach Steve."

"What is it?" He straightens his sunglasses.

My anxious face reflects back at me as I move closer. "I'd like to try a new position today."

"Oh, really. What position?"

"Goalie." I squeeze my hands.

"And why do you think you can play goalie?"

"I play catcher in baseball and I'm good at stopping the ball."

"Soccer is not baseball," he says sharply, and walks away like he's disgusted anybody would compare the two.

"I know they're not the same," I mumble. "Baseball's fun." I unclench my hands. I'm good with them. I'd like to use them.

CHAPTER 18

When we split up for our morning game, I'm still stuck on defense. Brady tightens the Velcro on his gloves and then stretches out his legs in the goal. He's wearing the neon-green goalie jersey rather than one of these ugly gold things.

Isaac's at forward on the other team and when the game starts, he chases down a long kick. I race over to get in front of him and bump his side. He lifts up his elbow and pushes me off.

"Keep your arm down." I beat him to the ball and control it with my right foot.

"Quit smashing into me." He bumps me with his hip and takes the ball from me.

I stay with him and steal it back and then pass to a teammate.

Isaac pushes me in the back.

"Keep your hands down," I say. "Remember, you can't use them in soccer."

One of the little guys on our team loses the ball and Isaac flies down the wing. I chase after him, but he beats me to the ball. I stay between him and the goal as he races to the corner.

Isaac stops, pivots, and fires a pass to the middle. Bowl Cut blasts it into the goal.

"Brady, you're giving him way too much space." Coach moves toward the goal. "You've got to react and cut down the angles."

Brady kicks the ball out of the net and bends down to pick dirt off his cleats as if that's the reason he was out of position.

Coach sets the ball in the center circle, and Scarface boots it. Bowl Cut gains possession and sends a high kick downfield. Isaac and I zoom after it.

The ball hits the ground and I kick it. But instead of the solid thunk of the ball, I catch Isaac's leg.

"Ahhhh!" He falls to the ground and grabs his knee.

Coach races in. "Give him room."

Players back up a step and Coach leans down. "Isaac?"

Isaac grimaces as he stretches out his leg and flexes his foot. He rubs the back of his calf.

"Are you okay?" Coach kneels down.

"I think so." Isaac reaches out his hands and two team-mates pull him up.

"Sorry." I walk over and pat him on the back.

He turns away from me and limps back with his team-mates.

"That's tripping and since it happened in the penalty area, it's a penalty kick." Coach scowls. "What were you do-ing, Kennedy?"

"Going for the ball." I walk away.

"Well, pay attention!" he shouts.

I hate this game.

Isaac lines up behind the penalty mark while we watch. He approaches the ball and drills a shot. Another goal.

"Brady, what are you doing?" Coach shouts. "You have to react quicker."

Brady turns his back and tightens his gloves.

"I've seen enough." Coach waves his hand. "Brady, switch places with Kennedy." I'm shocked to hear my name. Coach just chewed me out. Now he wants me to replace Brady.

"Hurry up, Kennedy." Coach points. "You said you wanted to play goalie. Here's your chance."

I run back to the goal. Brady glares at me as he slowly takes off the green jersey and goalie gloves and hands them to me. I put them on as fast as I can.

"Let's see some crisp passes and strong teamwork," Coach says.

I walk back and forth between the posts, and the goal seems huge. There's so much space to protect that I'm surprised soccer scores aren't twenty-nine to twenty-seven or something big like that.

Coach walks to the center circle. It's only seconds before everybody is going to be rushing at me, trying to get the ball past. I don't know anything about playing goalie. Why did I open my big mouth?

"Ready, Kennedy?" Coach calls.

"Ready." I try to sound confident, though I wish I could run right off the field.

I roll my arms to loosen up. At least on defense, you run around and burn off some of the energy.

Right away the ball comes down to our end. I move when the ball goes to the corner, but remind myself not to get out of position.

In a blur, a pass zips to the middle and I quickly move

left. I catch a flash of white and the ball is blazing toward me. I reach my arms out and hang on tight.

"Good save." Scarface comes back for the ball and I roll it out to him.

My first save. I didn't have time to think. I just reacted. And I got to use my hands.

Our forwards pass the ball back and forth, but don't manage any good shots on goal. Isaac leads a rush and passes to the center. Our defenders are slow to get back and Isaac rushes at me with the return pass.

I keep my eye on him all the way, but at the last instant he flicks a pass with his left foot to the middle. I dive back that way and Bowl Cut fakes a shot. He stops and passes to Isaac, who slams it into the wide-open net.

"Don't leave your feet, Kennedy," Coach calls.

"Three to nothing." Isaac raises his arms.

I retrieve the ball from the back of the net. I got totally faked out.

"One more goal," Coach shouts.

On the next rush, I focus on the ball but keep my eyes on the other players as well. Isaac shoots from the side, but I see it coming and make the save.

I boot the ball downfield and everybody chases after it. I step forward in the goal box and watch everybody moving around the field in a swirl of colors. I like the view from back here.

The church bells clang three times, meaning it's a quarter to twelve—fifteen minutes to lunch. The time's flown by.

I rub my hands together and prepare for the next rush. Just me back here. The last line of defense. I like being goalie.

CHAPTER 19

After lunch, Gig leads Isaac and me down the hill on the way to the soccer field. Two gardeners pull weeds in one of the flower beds. Wispy clouds float in the sky.

"No rain in sight," Gig says. "Great night for ghost hunting."

I shake my head. "I'm not going back out in those woods."

"Me neither," Isaac says.

"Are you girly girls scared?" Gig taunts.

"No." I slip on some sand but regain my balance. "We don't need to go back there."

"We've got to," Gig says. "If all three of us go, we'll outnumber the ghosts."

"What about Diego?" Isaac asks.

"He'll go," Gig says.

"No, he won't," I say. "Where is he anyway?"

"Hanging out with the other soccer stars," Isaac says. "He wanted us all to come to camp, but we hardly even see him."

"Yeah," I say. "The whole idea was to stick together. But we're on different teams, and I bet we'll be split up for the stupid tournament."

"How much do you want to bet?" Gig sticks out his hand.

"What?"

"I bet you one hundred bucks we'll be on the same team."

I look at him suspiciously. "What do you know that we don't?"

"So much," he sighs. "I don't even know where to begin."

At the field, kids swarm around the white board where the tournament teams are posted. I bite my lip. I hope I'm with at least one of my friends.

Gig grins at me.

"What's the matter with you?"

"Check the board, smart mouth." He points.

Isaac and I push into the crowd while Gig sits down and puts on his cleats. Isaac budges forward and I follow him. Scarface elbows me in the side and I push back.

"You and me." Isaac smiles at me. "We're together on the Cobras." He pulls me forward.

Isaac's name is right under mine. And two down is Spencer Milroy. "And Gig."

"Look at the bottom," Isaac says.

I scan the list. Diego Jimenez. I don't believe it. "Yes! We're all on the same team." I bump fists with Isaac and see Diego in back with the stars. He hasn't seen the board yet. He doesn't know he's not with them. How's he going to feel about that?

"Who else is with us?" Isaac asks.

I look back at the board. "Brady. He'll want to be goalie. And two kids I don't know, Eli and Brandon."

"That's us." Scarface steps forward with Bowl Cut. "I'm Eli and this is Brandon."

"Sorry." I hold up my hands. "I didn't know your names."

"Well, you should," Brandon says. "We've been playing together all week."

"We're teammates now," Isaac says. "For the tournament, we're all Cobras."

"We've got to tell Gig." I wave to Eli and Brandon. "See you on the field."

As Isaac and I rush off, Diego and his friends move toward the board. I don't tell him he's with us. He'll find that out soon enough.

"We're all together," Isaac says to Gig.

"On the same team," I add. "Can you believe it?"

Gig scrunches his lips together. "Good thing you skipped that bet."

"Wait a minute. You knew all along."

Gig keeps grinning like a clown.

"What did you do?" Isaac says. "Tell us."

"One word," Gig says.

"What?"

"Lauren."

"You got her to put us all on the same team?"

"I told you she likes me," Gig says. "And Coach Derek likes her, so she got him to do her a favor."

I look back at the board where Diego and the soccer stars crowd around it. He shakes his head. I'm sure he's disappointed he's stuck with us.

*I*n the first game of the tournament, I'm back again on defense with Brandon. I wish Coach Steve would listen to me about where I want to play.

Gig and Diego are forwards and already they're arguing.

"Pass the ball." Diego gets in Gig's face.

"I didn't see you," Gig shouts.

"Well, look for your teammates. Don't try to do it all by yourself."

Isaac steps between them and pushes them apart. "Knock it off, you two."

Our opponent, the Pythons, move into our end with a series of quick passes. I'm marking one of Diego's friends who's big and fast. He throws an elbow against my shoulder and races for the ball.

I rush to cut off his path and he kicks a pass to the center. I turn to see Brady slip and fall to the ground as the ball sails into the open net. One to zero. I could have done better than that. Anybody could have.

On the next possession, I pass to Brandon, who passes to Eli at midfield. He finds Diego, who fakes out a defender and rushes forward. He has a two-on-one break with Isaac and he fakes a shot that the goalie goes for. Diego passes to Isaac, who has a wide open net, but the ball skips off his foot, and he doesn't even get a shot off.

"My bad." Isaac taps his chest.

Diego hurries back after his man and gives him a bump. The Pythons pass the ball quickly and send a wave of players forward. They seem to be one step ahead of us, and the ball zips around in our end. Brady misses two more shots that he should have stopped, and we're down three to zero.

"Pick it up," Diego hollers. "Let's go."

I can tell he's frustrated. He's used to playing with stars, not losers like us.

CHAPTER

After dinner, I lie on my bed before the evening game. My legs hurt from all the running. In other sports, like baseball and football, you get to rest between plays. But with soccer, you keep moving all the time. Soccer players have to be in really good shape. I notice a bruise beginning to form on my right thigh. I don't even remember who gave me that.

I rub my eyes and try to clear my head. Gig got us all on the same team, but we didn't play like teammates. We were arguing and complaining. Maybe it would have been better to keep us separated. At least Diego, so he wouldn't get so frustrated whenever we miss a pass.

I sink down in the bed and close my eyes, but I'm brought back by the church bells ringing.

One.

Two.

Three—that means quarter to seven. I stagger out of bed, put on enough bug spray so that I smell like I've bathed in it, grab my cleats and shin guards, and head down to the field.

Gig and Isaac kick a ball back and forth and Gig waves me over. "Isaac says he'll go."

"Where?"

"To the chapel by the lake. Tonight. Ghost hunt."

"I said I'd go if Jackson did," Isaac corrects.

"We don't have to go back out there." I hold up my hands.

"We do too," Gig says. "We have to find them."

Diego's down by the goal in a circle with his friends. They're using their heads, knees, and feet to keep the ball in the air. He should be back here with us. We're his team-mates now.

"Let's get started, Cobras," Coach Steve calls. "Same positions as last game."

I bend down to double knot my laces. Why aren't we making some changes after getting blown out last game?

"Play hard. Play fair." Coach picks up the ball and takes it to the center circle.

I take my place on defense and glance at the goal. Brady jumps up and down like he's on a trampoline. That seems a weird way to get ready.

"Play tight defense," Diego yells down at us. "Don't give up any goals."

That's easy for him to say. He's not back here with waves of players rushing at him and a goalie who's no good. "Play good offense," I shout. "Score some goals."

Diego glares at me.

"You're the one who wanted us all here," I shout. "We should stick together."

"Here we go." Coach puts the ball in play.

Isaac controls it and passes to Diego. He weaves through three defenders and takes an awkward shot on goal. Gig was wide open on his left. Maybe he didn't see him. Or maybe he figures he can't trust us and needs to do it all on his own.

"Pass the ball," Gig hollers. "That's what you always tell me."

"Let's go," Isaac says. "Play together."

Eli steals the ball and passes ahead to Diego, who passes it to Isaac. He hesitates, then passes it back to Gig.

Gig loops a pass ahead to Diego, who chases it into the corner. He bumps and pushes with his defender and centers a pass that rolls all the way across the middle with nobody getting a foot on it.

"Come on," he hollers.

Back and forth we run. Our opponents, the Copperheads, score on a long shot that Brady should have stopped, but Diego evens the score on a beautiful fake. The game stays tied until Brady slips and lets in another easy goal.

"It's these shoes," he complains, but nobody, including him, believes that.

"**W**ake up." Gig's shaking me awake and standing next to him is Isaac. They're both dressed.

"Let me sleep." I roll over. "What time is it?"

"Five minutes to ghost hunt." Gig rips off my covers. "It's our last night at camp. We have to go now."

"You're crazy. I'm not going." I check my phone: 11:53.

"Yes, you are." Gig pulls me out of bed and Isaac helps me stand up. "We're all in this together."

"What if we get caught?"

"We're not going to get caught," Gig says.

Isaac guides me to my closet and I slowly pull on my pants.

"We need one more if we're all in this together," I say.

Gig looks at me. "What?"

"I'm not in if Diego isn't." I slip on my Go Strong T-shirt.

"He's sleeping," Isaac says.

"I was, too." I pull my sweatshirt over my head and grab my baseball hat and bug spray.

Gig waves to us and points to his mouth. We hear footsteps coming down the tile floor. Maybe it's Coach Derek on one of his nightly rounds.

When the footsteps are gone, Gig turns to us. "Okay, we'll get Diego." He turns the handle gently, and one by one, we step into the darkened hall.

The red EXIT sign dimly lights the way as we creep along to Room 352. We quietly open the door and spill into the room. On the bed, Diego's snoring loudly.

"How do you sleep with that chain saw?" Gig says to Isaac.

"What do you mean?" I interrupt. "You're louder than that."

"I don't snore!" Gig says.

"Keep it down," Isaac whispers.

The three of us stand over Diego like we're looking at a coffin at a funeral. I'm counting on him saying no so I can go back to bed.

"Diego." Gig pulls on his hand.

Nothing but snoring.

"Diego." I push his shoulder.

More snoring.

"Sleeping beauty." Isaac squeezes Diego's pinkie toe and he pops up.

"What?" Diego looks around.

"Ghost hunt," Gig says. "Grab your clothes."

Diego gets up, goes to his closet, and gets dressed like he's sleepwalking. Now all four of us are going into the woods for the ghost hunt, even though that's the last thing I want to do.

I've seen enough ghosts for one camp.

CHAPTER 21

Gig opens the door and we tiptoe down the hall. Maybe I should make some noise so Coach catches us. What would the punishment be anyway? Maybe we'd have to sit on the sideline for the last couple of games of the tournament tomorrow. Maybe we'd have to run some laps. Either of those would be better than going out there with ghosts.

Gig pushes open the door to the landing and we climb down the stairs.

"Where are we going?" Diego asks like he's finally woken up.

"We'd better not get caught," Isaac says.

"Be quiet or we *will* get caught." Gig opens the outside door and we all file through. He closes it slowly, but the click when it shuts sounds final, like we're locked out here and can't go back.

Gig leads us toward the church, and the moon casts spooky shadows. "Keep your eyes open for anyone else."

"Who else is going to be out here at midnight?" Isaac asks.

"That's what we're trying to find out," Gig says.

I breathe in the cool night air and stick my hands in my sweatshirt pocket and feel the can of bug spray. I spray some onto my hand and rub it on my exposed skin. "Anybody else want some of this?"

"Gig and I already put some on," Isaac says.

"I'll take a little," Diego says.

"Look." Isaac points.

Ahead of us someone is walking toward the Science Center.

"Over here." Gig pulls me behind an evergreen clump, and Isaac and Diego follow.

"What's he doing?" Diego whispers.

"Maybe he's a teacher working late."

"At midnight?" Isaac asks.

"Maybe he can't sleep." I hold still.

"Maybe you're an idiot," Gig says.

"Shhh," we all whisper. The teacher bends down and opens the door with his key card.

"Let's go this way." Gig turns down the path in front of the auditorium and we follow.

"How about we go by the girls' dorm?" Isaac says.

"No," Gig says firmly. "We're on a mission."

We follow the paved path down to the lake and stop at the beach. The lake is so still, it looks like a solid surface. The reflection of the moon is about as bright as it is in the sky.

I look up at the ceiling of stars. More stars than anyone could count. Being down here feels like enough of an adventure. "We're not going to see any ghosts tonight. Let's go back."

"No," says Gig. "We're going to find these ghosts together."

"Who chose him as leader?" Isaac leans close to me.

"He did," I say. "Who else would vote for him?"

Gig turns down the gravel path with Isaac and Diego behind him and me in the rear. I'd rather be in the middle. When something bad happens in a horror movie, it's always the first person or the last person. The middle is the safest place to be.

"Keep your eyes open," Gig says.

"Good idea," Isaac says. "Like we'd walk around out here with them closed."

I concentrate on the ground in front of me. The moon is like a spotlight that shines the way.

Ouuuu, ouuuu, woooo.

We all stop in our tracks.

Ouuuu, ouuuu, woooo. A haunting sound hangs in the air.

"Wha . . . what's that?" Diego says.

"Sounds like a wolf." I stare in the direction it came from.

"That's no wolf," Gig says. "It's the ghosts. They're trying to scare us."

I take a step back on the path. They're succeeding.

Ouuuu, ouuuu, woooo.

A shiver runs through me.

"Look." Isaac points to something small on the lake. "That's a loon calling."

"What's he doing up?" Diego asks.

"I don't know," I say. "He's probably wondering the same thing about us."

We follow the path up a hill and down by the lake.

"This is where Jackson and I saw the two ghosts last time." Gig stops. "Let's look for clues."

"What kind of clues do ghosts leave?" Diego asks.

"I don't know." Gig bends down. "But we're going to find them."

I follow Isaac down to the edge of the lake. "This is stupid," he says. "We're not going to find any clues."

"Look." Gig holds up a cigarette butt.

"What's that prove?" Isaac asks. "That ghosts smoke?"

"It's a clue," Gig says. "We're gathering clues."

"You don't have a clue," I say, and Isaac and Diego laugh.

"Let's go out to the chapel." Gig points to the spire. "Maybe we'll find something there."

The path drops down through a wet part and we move to the side to avoid the mud. A mosquito buzzes by my ear, and I slap at it and miss.

I'd like to go back, but if I turn around now I'd be in the woods by myself in the dark. I squeeze ahead of Diego so I'm not the last in line.

When we finally get to the chapel at the edge of the lake, it's bigger than I expected since it looks so small from the beach. Gig leads us up the rock steps and opens the wooden door. We step inside and the moon lights up the stained glass.

"Cool," Diego says.

"What do you think they use this for?" I look around at the cement floor.

"The college kids probably come out here to party," Gig says.

"Nah," Diego says. "You don't party in a chapel."

"Maybe it's for special ceremonies," Isaac says.

"Ghost ceremonies," Gig says. "Sacrifices."

Even though he's joking, it feels kind of creepy. I look out the window at the lake. Behind it the college buildings stand on the hill.

"Let's start back," Isaac says. "We've got two tournament games tomorrow."

"Today," I remind him. "It's already Friday."

"Yeah," Diego says. "Let's head back."

I know Gig wants to keep looking for clues, but even he knows when he's outvoted.

Walking back is easier. I know where the path goes and my eyes have adjusted better to the dark.

I even take the lead when Gig stops at the spot he found the cigarette butt. I keep an eye out for branches and roots and puddles of water and lead the way back to the beach.

"No ghosts," Isaac says.

"That doesn't mean they're not out here," Gig protests.

"Maybe you imagined them," Diego says.

"We didn't imagine them," I say. "Gig saw them. I saw

them. They were black and coming at us." I kick at the sand. I'm glad we didn't run into them tonight, but I don't want people doubting what we saw, either.

"Let's go to the girls' dorm now," Gig says.

"No," Diego says. "I'm going back."

"Me, too," I say.

"Me, three," Isaac adds.

"Look." Gig stops and points.

Ahead of us, on the sidewalk lined with trees, is a ghost. All in black, it's floating away from us.

I turn to look at Diego and Isaac and see the fear in their faces. I step back and turn to the beach.

"No," Gig says. "We're following it."

He steps forward and even though I don't want them to, my legs follow him. We all creep along the path and keep a safe distance behind the ghost. Gig waves at us to go faster, but I don't want to get any closer.

Suddenly the ghost stops and turns around.

My stomach feels like it's flipped over and I'm ready to die of fright. But then, out of the shadows, I see a white face and glasses.

"That's not a ghost," Diego says. "That's a monk."

"Good evening, gentleman." The non-ghost walks toward

us and adjusts his glasses. He's got a short beard and is wearing a long black robe.

"Good evening, Father," Diego says.

"I'm not a Father. I'm Brother Frederick, the night watchman," the monk says. "Are you gentlemen here for soccer camp?"

"Yes," I say. "We're just out exploring."

"Did you find what you were looking for?" Brother Frederick smiles.

"Yes," I say. "We did."

"Excellent," Brother Frederick says. "Have a good night."

"Thanks," I say as he walks away with his hands in the pockets of his black robes. He didn't chew us out or threaten to turn us in to Coach Derek. He didn't even tell us to go back to bed.

"You norks don't know the difference between a monk and a ghost." Diego shakes his head. "That's what you've been seeing all along."

"Well, they looked like ghosts," Gig says.

"Not quite." Isaac laughs.

"What's a nork?" I turn to Diego.

"A combination of a nerd and a dork."

"Nork, nork," Gig barks like a seal.

I feel a lot lighter as we walk back to our dorm even though I know Gig and I are going to hear about our fake ghosts for a long time.

That's okay. It's a relief to find out something isn't as scary as you think.

Chapter 22

When Gig, Isaac, and I arrive at the field on Friday morning, Diego's in the middle of an intense face-to-face with Coach Derek down by the goal.

"What do you think they're talking about?" I watch Diego move his hands as he talks.

"Diego's probably trying to switch to another team," Gig says.

"Yeah, one where he has a better chance to win," Isaac adds.

I bend down and adjust my socks over my shin guards. "That's not cool."

"Hey." Diego races over with a grin on his face.

"What?" I stand up. He shouldn't be so excited about ditching us.

"Coach says we can make some position changes for our game against the Diamondbacks."

"I want to stay at forward." Gig jumps up and down.

"I want to move to defense," Isaac says. "I'm better on defense."

"Let's try it," Diego says.

"I want to switch, too." I look over at the goal. "I want to play goalie."

Diego looks surprised. "Can you play goalie?"

"Yeah, I practiced there."

"He can't be worse than Brady," Gig says.

"Yeah, give him a chance," Isaac adds.

"Okay, I'll move Brady up front," Diego says. "Eli, too. He's got good speed. I'm going to switch to defense. If we don't give up goals, we've got a chance."

"Take your positions," Coach shouts.

I pull the neon-green jersey over my gray shirt and put on the goalie gloves. I shouldn't have doubted Diego like that.

I pace back and forth in front of the goal. After being out late last night, I expected to be tired, but I'm excited— excited to get my chance in goal. Diego and Isaac position themselves on defense, and Coach blows his whistle to start the game.

The Diamondbacks attack, but Isaac intercepts a pass and kicks it downfield. Gig chases after it in a whirl of arms and legs. He beats everyone to the ball and passes it to the center, but no one is there.

The Diamondbacks weave the ball our way and Diego pushes against a shorter player to take it away. The ball pops loose and Isaac rushes to get it. He gets cut off so he taps it back to me.

"Diego!" I holler and throw a long pass. He takes off along the sideline and passes to Brady. He finds Gig on the wing, who kicks the ball to the side and outruns a defender. He tries to center it, but the ball is blocked back toward midfield. The Diamondbacks rush our way, but I feel more confident with Isaac and Diego in front of me. Isaac stops the rush, but the ball goes off his foot past the end line.

The Diamondbacks line up for a corner kick.

"Isaac, Brandon, over here. Jackson, slide more to the middle." Diego's positioning people where he wants them.

I move to the middle and survey the Diamondbacks. Their tallest guy is whispering to the person next to him. I bite down on my lip. I wish I'd brought some bubble gum to chew.

The corner kick flies in and the tall guy jumps and heads the ball at the net. I see the whole thing coming and catch the ball like it's a weak throw in dodgeball. I pivot and roll the ball out to Diego.

Back and forth we go. We don't get much going on offense, but we don't give up any goals, either. It's just like Diego said: If we don't give up goals, we've got a chance.

I relax when the ball goes down to Gig, Brady, and Eli at the other end, but most of the time it's in our zone and players are coming at me. Diego and Isaac play tough in front of me and the Diamondbacks are not getting many good shots.

Suddenly a blast comes from the outside. I crouch low to stop it and hold on tightly.

"Nice stop, Jackson," Brandon shouts.

I roll the ball out to Diego, but he lets it get stolen, and two Diamondbacks rush at me. I shade to the right, but the tall guy boots a pass to the middle. Isaac is looking the other way and the ball hits the back of his shoulder and ricochets toward the goal. I dive to stop it but I'm too late.

"My bad." Isaac puts his hands to his head like he can't believe it.

"My fault," I say. I still should have stopped it.

"No, it was my fault," Diego says. "I never should have lost the ball in my own end like that. I should have cleared it."

I kick the ball out of the net. We'd finally been playing good together so it hurts to give up a cheap goal like that.

Once the ball's in play, Gig tries to advance it on offense, but he's outnumbered and gets pushed off the ball. The Diamondbacks keep the pressure on, but I stop three more shots, and Diego and Isaac clear the zone.

"Five more minutes," Coach Derek calls the time remaining.

"I'm going to switch to offense to help Gig," Diego says. "We need a goal." He races down and sends Brady back. I look over at Isaac. We've got to do the best we can without Diego back here.

A ball bounces our way and Isaac hesitates before going after it. Brady's not sure what to do, either, as three Diamondbacks rush at us. The tall guy passes to the middle and receives the ball back on a give-and-go. He boots a rocket that smacks off the pole but rebounds right back to him. He kicks it at the wide-open net as I dive to get back. The ball zips past me for their second goal.

"Good try," Isaac says.

I throw the ball out. The ball hitting the post and bouncing right back to him was a bad break.

On offense, Gig weaves between defenders and finds Diego, who pushes his way to the middle. Defenders surround him, but somehow he flicks a pass to the side. Gig races in and kicks a shot.

The ball flies to the goal. It's going to be close. The goalie scrambles to get back, and the ball sails over his head and into the net.

"GOOOOOAL!" I yell.

"GOOOOOAL!" Gig stretches out his arms like he's a plane.

"GOOOOOAL!" Isaac shouts, and races downfield.

I race down and chest bump Gig. "We scored. We got a goal."

"Time!" Coach hollers.

I wipe the sweat from my face. Two to one. We only lost by a goal and we worked better together. But best of all I finally earned the position I want—goalie.

Chapter 23

At lunch, the four of us return to the same table we sat at on Sunday when we first came to camp. That seems so long ago, like a different year.

"How did you get two?" Diego points to Gig's cheeseburgers.

"Stephanie knows I like cheeseburgers."

"Who's Stephanie?" Isaac asks.

"She works on the west line next to Jackie."

"You know the food service workers by name?" I ask.

"Of course," Gig says. "They're the most important people here. I tell them how good the food is. They like hearing what we like and what we don't."

"These cheeseburgers are great," Diego says.

"Then tell them." Gig jams some fries in his face.

"That was a nice goal," Isaac says to Gig. "You and Diego

worked well together. Maybe you should be up front all the time."

"But we need Diego back on defense," I say. He knows what to do to cut down their chances.

"We need two Diegos," Isaac says. "One up front and one back on defense."

"Three," I say. "The third one can play midfielder."

"Four," Gig says. "If we had four Diegos we could beat anybody."

Diego smiles and gets up. "I need another cheeseburger."

"But we've only got one Diego," I say. "We need to figure out where to put him."

"Offense," Gig says.

"Defense," Isaac says.

"I agree with Isaac," I say. "If they don't score, we've got a chance. That's what Diego says."

"Let's ask him when he gets back," Gig says. "He should decide."

Across the room Angela sits with Carlos and Crystal. Isaac hasn't been sitting with her lately or hanging out with her. I catch his eye. "What's up with Crystal?"

"Nothing," he says.

"Why?"

"I don't know. She wanted to do stuff and then she didn't. I don't understand girls."

"Me neither." I think about how focusing on Angela pulled me away from the guys. "We don't need them."

"Except for Lauren," Gig says. "We needed her to get us on the same team."

Diego finally comes back with another cheeseburger and a mound of french fries.

"What took you?" I ask.

"The line was long."

"You don't have to wait in line," Gig says. "Stephanie lets me come right to the front."

"Diego," Isaac interrupts. "Do you think it's better if you play defense or offense?"

"Defense," Diego says.

"I told you," I tell Gig.

"Carlos's team scores a lot of goals," Diego says. "They've won three straight and Angela says he's been bragging about how they're going to crush us and be the champs."

"I'd love to crush him," Gig says.

"Me, too." I look over to where Carlos is talking with Crystal and she's squeaking in a high-pitched giggle.

"They're tough," Diego says. "Their games haven't even been close."

After lunch the four of us walk around the campus. Black-eyed Susans bloom in a bed in front of the auditorium.

"I like this place," Diego says.

"Would you go to college here?" Isaac asks.

"I don't know if I'm going to college," Diego says. "My uncle has a full-time job waiting for me on his roofing crew when I finish high school."

"You're smart," Isaac says. "You should go to college."

"Yeah," Gig adds. "Lots of jobs are easier than roofing."

"Would you go here?" I ask Isaac.

"Too quiet," he says. "I want to be in a big city like New York or Chicago."

"What about you, Gig?"

"I *was* going to join the army after high school."

"Was?"

"Yeah, hearing my dad's stories about training camp makes it sound hard. The drill instructors yell at you. People are always telling you what to do. And worst of all, Dad says the food's not that good."

"You like the food here," Isaac says. "Maybe you should go here."

"I don't know," Gig says. "I hadn't thought about going to college. But you're right. Food will be a big part of my decision."

"Look." Diego points at two monks and opens his mouth wide and makes his eyes big. "Ghosts."

We all burst out laughing.

CHAPTER 24

"**H**ow many games have you won?" Carlos asks me as we take the field.

"None," I mumble as I tighten my gloves.

"How many?" He pulls a yellow pinnie over his Manchester United jersey.

"Zero." I'm sure he knows we're winless and is rubbing it in.

"We've won three. You've lost three. We should beat you by six goals."

I turn my back on him. His math doesn't make any sense.

"Hey, Carlos." Gig runs up. "How are you going to be able to run?"

"What do you mean?"

"Isn't it hard to move with your head so big?"

"Losers," Carlos says.

"What did you say you are?" Gig shoots back.

Coach Derek blows the whistle. "Let's get started."

Immediately Carlos's team, the Vipers, advances the ball. They are quicker than any team we've faced and pass the ball confidently.

"Get back, Isaac," Diego yells.

Behind Isaac, Carlos races to the ball. As soon as he gets it, he pivots and boots a pass. Diego lunges to kick it away, but it skips past his outstretched foot.

I move to the side of the goal. Adam Waldman, the hard-core kid Gig doesn't like, takes two steps and winds up to blast a shot. At the last second, he slips a pass to Carlos, who slams the ball into the open net.

"One to zero," Carlos says. "This is going to be so easy."

"Shut up." I kick the ball out of the net.

Diego walks over and slaps me on the back. "Don't worry. We'll get it back."

"Let's get another one," Waldman hollers. "Let's show them how fast we can score."

Gig controls the ball at midfield. He tries to advance it but is surrounded by defenders, and the ball is stripped from him.

Carlos leads the rush downfield and this time Isaac stays

back. Carlos passes to Waldman, but Diego takes it away from him and clears it to Brandon, who sends it downfield to Eli. One of the Vipers swoops in but makes a lazy cross-field pass.

Gig bursts through and steals it, setting up a one-on-one chance with the goalie. He moves left, stops, and sizzles a shot just inside the right post. It's good.

"GOOOOOAL!" I yell all the way down the field.

Gig raises his arms and runs back toward us. For someone who claims he doesn't like soccer, he's good.

"One to one," I call loud enough for Carlos to hear. "Tie game."

"Beginner's luck," he says.

"Great play, Gig." Diego bumps his fist.

"Quit celebrating like you've never scored a goal in your life," Waldman sneers.

"We can celebrate however we want." Isaac steps up to him. "Cobras, Cobras." He claps his hands.

The game moves up and down the field. Carlos and his teammates pressure our goal, but Isaac and Diego push them outside, and I make some big saves. On offense, Gig and Eli do their thing and the defenders scramble to keep up with them.

With six minutes left in the game, Carlos leads another rush. He fakes a pass and fires a shot. I get a hand on it, but the ball bounces right back to him. He kicks the rebound before I move over to cover the open area and it skids into the goal.

"Two to one." He raises his arms and runs to his team-mates.

I retrieve the ball from the net. I should have gotten two hands on it to hang on.

"Let's get it back." Isaac claps.

Gig runs all the way down to us. "Diego, you've got to come up front with me."

"I can't," he says. "I have to stay back here."

"We've got to go for it," Gig says.

"He's right." I step up. "We need a goal. We'll do our best back here. Go up front with Gig and Eli and get us a goal."

Diego frowns. He can't believe we'll be okay back here without him.

"Get up there." I wave him away. "Send Brady back."

Isaac walks over and puts his hand on my shoulders. "We have to stop them for six minutes."

"Yeah." I adjust the Velcro on my gloves. Six minutes feels like a really long time.

As soon as the ball's in play, Carlos and his teammates storm our end. Isaac steals the ball, but loses it to Carlos. He fires a pass to Waldman, who passes it back. Carlos has me one-on-one and sizes me up. He fakes a kick as I step out toward him. Then he blazes a rocket at the left corner.

I leap and get my hand on it and punch it past the net.

"Great save." Isaac rushes back and bumps fists.

"Way to go, Jackson!" Gig hollers.

"You're keeping us in this!" Diego shouts.

Even Coach Derek joins in from the sideline. "Nice save, Kennedy."

I chase down the ball and wipe my forehead. That was close. I need to be ready at all times.

On offense, Diego controls a pass and flips it back to Eli, who passes to Gig. He squeezes through two defenders with his whirligig moves and passes back to Eli. Eli shoves past his guy and skips the ball over to Gig, who's got a shot.

He winds up, but passes back to Diego, who blasts the ball home.

"GOOOOOAL! GOOOOOAL! GOOOOOAL!" We all yell and race around the field like chickens with our heads cut off.

"GOOOOOAL! GOOOOOAL! GOOOOOAL!" We all pile on top of Diego.

On the sideline, Coach checks his watch. "Two minutes left. Don't celebrate too early."

Isaac grabs me and pulls me up. "Come on."

"We've still got to hold them," Brady says as the three of us run down to our end.

"Go all out." Coach moves to the center circle. "Leave everything on the field."

Carlos controls the ball and barrels downfield. Gig and Diego try to slow him, but he pushes through them and passes to Waldman on the side. Waldman fakes to the middle, spins around, and leaves Isaac sprawling. He passes back to Carlos, who steams toward the goal.

Me and him. He glances up and smirks. I move forward to cut down the angle and he keeps coming at me. He draws his leg back and I slide to the side. The ball blasts off his foot and I dive to my right. I stretch my arm out as far as it will go but can't quite reach it. The ball sails past, but bangs off the post.

I'm laid out on the ground as I turn to see Waldman line up the rebound. There's no way I can get back over to that side of the goal.

Waldman grins as he kicks, but out of nowhere Brady slides in front to block and the ball rolls out of bounds.

"Way to go, Brady!" Diego hollers.

"You saved us." I point at Brady.

"Corner kick!" Carlos hollers. Waldman chases down the ball and runs to the corner.

I position myself in goal. Two minutes must be up by now.

Gig and Diego hurry back to provide as much defense as possible.

"Over here." Diego positions Isaac in front of Carlos and Gig behind him. Diego shadows him, too. He doesn't want Carlos to get the game winner.

Waldman curls the corner kick toward the front of the goal and everything slows down. Diego bumps Carlos with his hip, but Carlos still outjumps everybody and gets his head on the ball.

I slide to my left. Hang on. Hang on, I remind myself.

The ball comes closer and I reach to grab it and smother it against my chest.

Coach blows his whistle. "That's the game. Final score, two to two."

Carlos buries his face in his hands, and Waldman rips off his pinnie.

I stand in the goal with my arms wrapped around the ball, and my teammates swarm toward me.

"Cobras. Cobras. Cobras."

"Two to two," I yell. "We win."

And then I'm knocked to the ground with everybody piling on top.

A tie never felt so much like a victory.

Chapter 25

Diego joins us as we sit in the grass with all our gear in a pile waiting for Isaac's dad to pick us up.

Gig turns to Diego. "Did you see the look on Carlos's face after you scored?"

"How could I?" Diego says. "You all jumped on top of me."

"He couldn't believe it," Isaac says.

"But did you see the look?" Gig says.

"No." I sit up. "What did he look like?"

"Like he saw a ghost."

We all burst out laughing.

"Three losses and a tie," Isaac says. "We didn't win any games."

"Yeah, but we didn't lose to Carlos." I shake my head.

"Besides, the three of us don't even play soccer. We just came here for Diego."

"You play soccer now," Diego says.

"You won't believe it," Gig says, "but I kind of like soccer."

"Me, too," Isaac says. "I can see why so many people play it."

"And I like playing goalie," I say.

"But I'm not going to be on a team or anything," Gig says.

"Besides, we've got football coming up in three weeks," I say.

"Three weeks?" Isaac looks at me. "That's all?"

"Yeah, it's only two and half weeks until school starts."

"Sixteen days." Gig sticks out his tongue. "Then it's off to Longview Middle School Prison."

Nobody says anything. I imagine a huge metal gate clanging shut. Camp's actually been a nice break from worrying about Longview.

"My uncle said to be ready for Spirit Day," Gig says.

"What's that?" I ask, even though I don't really want to know.

"The day each year that eighth graders can make you do anything they want. Anything!"

"My sisters never mentioned that," Isaac says.

"They didn't go to Longview," Gig says. "And besides, Spirit Day is a lot worse for boys."

I stretch out my legs. Eighth graders are probably making horrific plans for us right now.

"Make sure to stay out of the bathroom if eighth graders are in there," Diego says. "My brother says that's where trouble starts."

"What if you have to go?" Isaac asks.

"Stay away from the bathroom if eighth graders are in there," Diego repeats.

"That's what drinking fountains are for." Gig laughs.

"At least all four of us will be together," I say.

"Yeah," Isaac says. "We'll stick together at school and on the field."

"We're all playing football together." Gig smacks his hand.

"I've never gone out for it," Diego says. "My mom thinks football's dangerous. She doesn't want me to play."

"Moms are like that," Gig says. "You have to play."

"Yeah." I nod. "We need you."

"And we all came to soccer camp," Isaac says.

"Okay. Okay." Diego raises his hands. "I'll try to convince her."

"Not try," I say. "You will." I bump fists with him and Gig and Isaac. "We're all going to play football. We're sticking together. All four of us."

Acknowledgments

*T*hank you to Gabe and Joachim Hossick-Schott and the soccer players at Pearl Park and Ned Rousmaniere and his team at Matthews Park for providing tips and strategies.

Thank you to Liz Szabla, Jean Feiwel, Elizabeth Fithian, Rich Deas, Caroline Sun, and everybody at Feiwel and Friends. I love being on the team.

Thank you to my all-star agent, Andrea Cascardi, who knows goals, and the KTM writers who cover the field.

Thank you to everyone at Echo Park Elementary School, especially Sally Soliday, Paula Kranz, Judy Zarn, and to teachers Dan Dudley and Kim Coleman and their students for their keen insights.

Thank you to Principal Kim Hill Phelps, my own grade school classmate, and everyone at Flynn Elementary School, particularly Cheryl Lawrence and Matt Wigdahl and their fifth-grade students for their sharp suggestions.

And thank you again to Doug Fraser for his outstanding cover. Two-for-two.